LEFTOVERS

A NOVEL

ARTHUR WOOTEN

GALAXIAS PRODUCTIONS

LEFTOVERS: A NOVEL

Galaxias Productions
200 West 90ᵗʰ Street Suite 9B
New York, NY 10024

All rights reserved.

ISBN: 978-0-9850529-2-8

Graphic Art by: Bud Santora

DEDICATION

For my father, Dr. Arthur L. Wooten, Jr.,
a true pioneer in the plastics industry

CONTENTS

ONE

A CHARMED LIFE

In 1954, Vivian Lawson Hayes was the most famous and re-
spected wife and homemaker in the picturesque New England
town of Abbot, Massachusetts. Actually, the entire eastern sea-
board looked up to her. And, although a poll had yet to be taken,
it was suspected that she was the most emulated and admired
woman in the United States. In fact, women around the world
who had never even heard of Vivian Lawson Hayes or knew that
she existed wanted to be her. That's how perfect she was.

She was so revered that the new television show, *The Perfect
Wife*, airing out of Boston, featured her in their season's premiere
episode. Following Vivian around her house and hometown for 24
hours, the viewers had a rare glimpse into this domestic engineer's unique, if not bizarre, world.

As the camera crew pulled up to Vivian's Cape Cod house that
was lovingly wrapped in silver-weathered cedar shake siding and
maintained in pristine condition, she appeared at the front door
waving enthusiastically. Dressed in a Christian Dior black silk
cocktail dress, 3-inch black stiletto heels, and her shiny chocolate
brown hair exquisitely spun into a fashionable French twist,
Vivian treated the audience to a quick tour of her perfectly land-

scaped and manicured yard that she designed and maintained herself. It was springtime and the properly pruned rhododendrons, dogwoods and azaleas were magnificently in full bloom.

Sitting in the driveway was an unobtainable sparkling black 1955 Cadillac convertible. She hopped in and the television crew tried to keep up with her as she sped down the street. She zipped through the town of Abbot with the top down and not a single strand of Vivian Lawson Hayes' hair blew out of place. Crowds of people lined the streets, waving to her as though they had known she was coming and had planned a parade.

Back at the house she courteously escorted the cameras into her inner sanctum. When asked where her children were she proudly announced that her six-year-old boy, John, and eight-year-old girl, Mary, were safely tucked away at the La Clairière boarding school in Villars, Switzerland. Vivian also admitted to speaking seven languages, proficiently.

With a cigarette in one hand and a cocktail in the other, she showed off the state-of-the-art appliances in her kitchen and reminded us that the perfect homemaker is an accomplished chef, mastering the ability to cook foods from all over the world. But with her creative flair and snagging just a few extra minutes from her busy day, Vivian took that one step farther and had created her own cuisine, Vivianese. A cookbook was soon to follow.

As she led the viewers through the living room, pointing out the expensive heirloom furniture and museum quality artwork, she reminded all women that it is the duty of the "supreme wife" to run her household like clockwork. And although she was the general manager, the president was, and always would be, her husband. She ran a beautiful and tight ship, but her most important job was to serve him. He worked hard to provide for her and their children, so the least she could do was speak in a soothing tone when he came home from a hard day at work. Vivian always made sure that she had a cocktail waiting for him, slid off his shoes and handed him his slippers and pipe, allowing him to relax and unwind before she added the finishing touches to the night's candlelit dinner.

When asked where her husband Paul was that evening, she was proud to announce that as Captain of the Abbot Police Department, it was demanded of him to work 24-hour shifts, sometimes days, even weeks at a time. And without missing a beat she then rattled off the house rules for herself with an oversized but slightly rigid smile.

"I never judge Paul's motives or actions," she declared as she pulled a tissue out of her dress pocket and unconsciously started to shred it. "If he's late for dinner or even stays out all night, I consider that trivial compared to what he must have endured at work during the day. He is master of the house and I have no right to question him. Also, if I'm suffering from dizzy spells, headaches, backaches or even if I'm choking, I rack these complaints up as imaginary nuisances on my part and never bother him with them." Noticing the bits of the destroyed tissue on the floor, she smiled hard at the camera and quickly picked them up.

When it was time for Vivian Lawson Hayes to retire for the evening, the cameras followed her up the stairs and into her serene bedroom. The décor certainly had a woman's sensibility, but she had been careful to add masculine touches to make sure that her husband didn't feel threatened by her feminine mystique.

She disappeared into her dressing room for a brief moment and reemerged wearing a chic, floor length, black chiffon negligee slit up the front with billowing butterfly sleeves and then glided over to the queen size bed. She slipped in between her crisply ironed imported Egyptian cotton sheets that sported her initials and laid her head gently down onto a pillow, wearing a full face of make-up and her hair still perfectly French twisted. And then, as everyone watched, she remarkably fell asleep on cue.

Just as she was about to awaken and share with all her en suite European-style bathroom with gold-plated fixtures, including a bidet that had been shipped over from Paris and once used by

Coco Chanel, she heard the sound of running water. Vivian tossed slightly from side to side as its intensity increased. It became so extreme that it actually created a roar, but Vivian Lawson Hayes didn't wake up. Instead, beads of sweat shockingly appeared on her wrinkle-less forehead as the terrifying sound of gushing water became unbearable.

Finally, Vivian's eyes opened wide. As if paralyzed, she watched in horror as she saw the ceiling above bulge from the weight of tons of water. Her perfect house, her perfect life was beginning to crack. Plaster chipped off, support beams gave way and suddenly Vivian was assaulted by shards of splintering wood and gallons of water. Everything went black. Drowning, she struggled to determine which way was up and swam against the current, desperate to reach the surface for air.

"Viv?"

She thought she heard her husband call out to her.

"Viv!"

Knowing he was there, somewhere, she reached out for him.

"Vivian!" Paul shouted from the shower.

Startled, Vivian bolted upright in bed and gasped for air. Drenched in flop sweat, she was wearing a Sears and Roebuck flannel nightgown with a faded flower print that was frayed around the collar. Her mousey brown hair was knotted and damp. Completely disoriented, she wasn't sure whether she had just experienced a dream, a nightmare, a panic attack, or all three simultaneously.

Paul screamed, again. "Vivian, there's no goddamn soap in here!"

She glanced at the alarm clock and was shocked at how late she had overslept. She shot out of bed and ran into the bathroom. Hardly the award winning en suite she had dreamt of, the stained porcelain sink sat in a chipped and rotted wood vanity. She wrestled with the cabinet door below, kicked it open and grabbed a bar of soap. When she stuck her hand around the shower curtain she briefly saw her husband's naked body.

At age 27, Paul Hayes was sexier looking and in better shape than the day he had married Vivian, five years earlier. His black wavy hair was going prematurely gray at the temples and somehow his light blue eyes were shifting into a haunting grayish white.

Vivian slipped her nightgown up over her head and examined herself in the mirror. Her fingers gently touched her non-existent eyebrows, then the corners of her light brown eyes, tracing the crow's feet that seemed to have appeared just within the past year. Thinking she looked older than her 25 years, she frowned, making the sides of her thin nose crinkle causing it to look more pinched than it was. She slid her hands down to her breasts, which were hardly large enough to cup in her hands and then turned sideways and examined her stomach.

Over the years she had accepted the strange thin scar that encircled her waist but was careful not to touch it. She turned her body to the other side and smiled, pleased at how flat her tummy was. But then weight gain was never an issue for her. Contrary to many of her female friends, when under stress she didn't overeat. Quite the opposite. In fact, her under-eating bordered on starvation. Food for Vivian was a reward. But she never was sure when she deserved it.

For a split second she considered joining Paul in the shower. If they were serious about having a child, they were going to have to have more sex. But not sure of what his reaction would be, she rushed out of the bathroom.

Lying on a threadbare wingback chair was Vivian's go-to nylon dress that she had nicknamed the "uniform". Inherited from her closest friend, Babs Parker, Vivian loved it because it was incapable of wrinkling; hence she was prone to wearing it several days in a row. And although only two years old, this once vibrant and stylish short sleeved dress with an orange geometric pattern was fading as quickly as Vivian's weight. She threw the tent over her head and knowing how long Paul would spend primping in the mirror, she hoped she had enough time to make sure that everything was just right. She went over to the nightstand, opened the drawer and took out a small gift-wrapped box and stuffed it into the pocket of her dress.

In her haste to rush downstairs, she slammed the drawer shut, causing a book to fall off from the table onto the floor. The cover read:

The Perfect Wife

A Guide For The Married Woman

Paul stepped out of the shower and listened for a moment. Sensing that she had left the bedroom, his shoulders relaxed and he smiled at himself in the bathroom mirror.

"Hey, beautiful," he whispered as he lathered shaving cream onto his face.

Like Vivian, Paul Hayes was also an Abbot "townie". All natives were labeled that unless they were either enrolled in or associated with the village's only current industry, the all-boys boarding school, Talbot Academy.

Paul was the youngest of four sons. He and his family once lived above his father Oscar's barbershop, located on Acorn Street just off Main. The men who trickled into the place and lingered for hours weren't necessarily getting just a haircut and a shave. If one were to use the phone booth against the back wall and knew just where to lean his body weight, a secret door would open, inviting him into the illegal pool hall and bookie joint that Oscar ran.

Fed up with her husband's gambling and womanizing ways and realizing that she had no influence over her uncontrollable delinquent boys, Paul's mother left town one Sunday evening and was never heard from again.

This was the only life Oscar knew, but that didn't necessarily mean that he wanted his sons to follow in his footsteps. When Oscar noticed Paul's athletic potential he encouraged his youngest to try out for the teams and by the time he was just a freshman, Paul was officially labeled "Harry High School". Eventually he became the first-string quarterback for the football team in fall, captain and point guard for the basketball squad in winter and a sprinter and long jumper for the track team in spring. Paul was the golden boy and everyone knew it, including himself.

The only thing he was lacking was intelligence. And it wasn't until he was held back in school a second time in his sophomore year that he even noticed Vivian Lawson. As a student she made straight A's and was always buried in a book, volunteering for the prom committee, of which she never attended, or supporting the Humanities Club. And although she wasn't popular, athletic, or pretty enough to be a cheerleader, she was allowed to join the Pep Club. Like all the girls at Abbot High she had a mad crush on Paul Hayes and when attending rallies, Vivian consciously projected her high-pitched voice directly at him, shouting cheers that sent annoying shivers throughout his entire body.

Everyone in town knew that the Lawsons were the wealthy owners of the Lawson Woolen Mills. Even though the factories had closed their doors for the final time ten years earlier, the family still had more money than they knew what to do with. And when William Lawson, Vivian's father, died of a heart attack in 1947, when Vivian was 18 years old, it was assumed that she, being his only child, would become heiress apparent. Although Paul had barely half a brain, he was smart enough to know that he wasn't going to make a living playing professional sports. But it was Oscar who came up with the idea that Paul should court Vivian.

Unfortunately for father and son, they discovered after Paul had married Vivian that William Lawson had died without drawing up his will. All of his money was left to his wife, Irene. Disappointed in her daughter's choice of husband but eager to get her out of her hair, she offered Vivian her blessings and but a tiny portion of the gargantuan inheritance.

~ ~ ~

Paul looked at himself in the mirror again as he lovingly shaved his face. "Hello smarmy," he cooed. He had recently heard a woman call him that when he made a pass at her while walking his beat through the center of town and being as smart as he was, he took it as a compliment.

A loud clash of pots and pans echoed up to the bathroom from the kitchen. Paul winced at the sound and cut himself with the razor. "Damn her!"

Vivian was a terrible cook and an even worse housekeeper. But one couldn't blame her. She had grown up in a massive brick mansion within a household with not one, but four maids. Maid 1 did the heavy cleaning like the washing of windows, waxing of floors and polishing of silver. Maid 2 did the light cleaning and the laundry. Maid 3 was the cook and Maid 4 attended to Mrs. Lawson's personal needs and grooming.

Vivian was not allowed to do any chores. Nor was she allowed to speak to the help. But she did call them by their numbers. Not because she was insolent or even being creative, it was what her mother called them. And whenever Mrs. Lawson was far off in her wing of the house or out for the day to shop or play bridge with her friends, Vivian would try to strike up conversations with any one of the numbers. Not because they were friendly or even interesting. Vivian was simply lonely. On occasion, it was Maid 3 who would permit Vivian to sit on a stool and watch her cook, but she was forbidden to say a word.

Most young girls, brought up amidst such wealth, were sent off to highbrow European boarding schools by their mothers. Or at the very least, they were polished and perfected at local charm academies. But not Vivian. Her mother, Irene, resented her existence. Never having wanted any children at all, she didn't refer to her daughter as a surprise or even an accident. In her eyes, Vivian was a mistake. And consequently, she ignored her child as much as she could.

Now married to Paul, Vivian looked back upon her childhood and the way she was brought up with disgust and condemnation and was seriously trying to teach herself how to be a normal housewife.

With her unwashed hair haphazardly pinned up out of her face with a few bobby pins, Vivian paused for a moment at the bottom of the staircase to see if she could hear Paul and then rushed back into the kitchen to study a cookbook. On the counter was a bowl of eggs while a pot of water sat on her massive Wedgewood gas stove.

She flipped through the book, eyed a page and then put it down on the counter. She hesitated a moment before walking over to the stove, then stood as far away from it as possible while still trying to see if the water was boiling. Top of the line when made in the early 1930s, this culinary dinosaur actually frightened Vivian to death.

~ ~ ~

At the age of ten and hungry for her mother's affection, Vivian wanted to surprise her on her birthday with breakfast in bed. Early in the morning, before anyone was up and the cook had entered the kitchen, she put on her favorite Sunday dress with matching red plastic belt and was eager to make pancakes, all on her own. Although she remembered the necessary ingredients, she was a bit creative when it came to the measurements of each item. And after enthusiastically mixing it all together the kitchen looked like a war zone, the battle fought with eggs, flour and milk.

With both hands she muscled the heavy cast iron skillet up onto the gas stove, poured all of the batter into the pan making one large disk and then turned the burner's knob on full blast. She had watched Maid 3 do this every time she lit the stove but when she reached for the box of matches, they were empty. She leisurely searched the kitchen for more. Finally she found them and struck the first stick against the sulfur; the next thing she remembered was being driven to the hospital in an ambulance.

The oven had exploded. The skillet flew towards Vivian, hitting the side of her skull and knocked her out as the fire ignited her dress. Made of light cotton, it disintegrated in an instant and she suffered first and second degree burns. Remarkably, the only scar that remained was the one made round her waist when the belt she had been wearing melted to her skin. Needless to say, this fueled her life-long hatred for belts. All the hair on her body was singed off and Vivian's eyebrows never grew back.

And although the house escaped with just smoke damage, her mother's kitchen was completely destroyed. Suffice it to say, it was not a happy day for either mother or daughter. In fact, Vivian's mother never forgave her and never missed an opportunity to rub this disaster in her daughter's face, even as an adult. Vivian often wondered which her mother valued more, her beloved dream kitchen, which was expensive but easy to replace, or her daughter's life.

~ ~ ~

So Vivian's fear of gas stoves was quite understandable. The Wedgewood was monstrous. It was equipped with six burners, two metal panel covers, a large roasting oven, a separate pastry oven which would never be used, a broiler, a griddle, built-in spice racks with no spices and a warming drawer which she kept her house slippers in during the winter months. And now, 15 years after that disastrous morning and with great trepidation, Vivian found herself struggling to create yet another special breakfast.

Her eyes darted to the teapot-shaped wall clock and knew she had to fly. Vivian opened a bottle of vinegar and splashed some into the pot of boiling water and then picked up an egg. She timidly knocked the shell against the edge of the bowl and nothing happened. She tapped it again with no results. She hit it harder and her hand crushed the entire egg, splattering it onto the front of her dress. She wiped it off with her hands and then cracked one more egg, gently letting it slip into the boiling water. Proud of herself, she wiped the sweat off of her brow with her forearm and then cracked another egg and slipped it in.

She reached over to the toaster and pushed two slices of bread down. Then she ran to the refrigerator and took out a glass bowl full of cut up fresh fruit, which was covered with waxed paper and held on with a rubber band. Keeping her distance, she took a quick peek at the eggs in the pot and then pulled the waxed paper off the bowl of fruit. Suddenly, the rubber band shot off and snapped Vivian in the face.

"Ah, geez," she moaned as her hand went up to her cheek.

"Vivian?" Paul hollered from upstairs. "Where's my tie?"

"On your tie rack!" she yelled back, shaking her head.

Looking at the clock again, she spooned the fruit salad onto a plate as the bread popped up. She grabbed an open can of deviled ham and smeared it onto the toast and threw it onto the plate. Vivian then took a slotted spoon and fished out a poached egg and made an attempt at landing it on top of the ham. She placed the whole mess on the table and studied the plate.

"I forgot the Hollandaise," she grumbled as she punched her thigh and grabbed an orange. She slit it in half and jammed it onto a reamer and twisted with all her might. She juiced the other half, dumped it into a glass and set it on the table.

She poured a cup of coffee and set it next to the juice as she heard Paul coming down the stairs. Beyond excited, she reached into her pocket and took out the small wrapped present and preciously placed it next to the plate of food.

Vivian quickly fumbled in her pocket again and pulled out a tube of lipstick and smeared it across her mouth. As Paul turned the corner and entered the kitchen wearing his policeman's uniform she spun around and smiled but he didn't make eye contact.

He picked up the glass of juice and downed it. "I'm late."

Without acknowledging the plate of food or the gift, he walked out of the kitchen.

Thrown, Vivian wondered if this breakfast had blown up in her face too. She grabbed the present and rushed into the hall just as he was opening the front door.

"Paul," she said, touching his arm.

He stopped as she stretched up to kiss him on the mouth but he only allowed her his cheek.

Deflated, she watched him as he made his way down their cracked cement walkway overgrown with weeds, to his brand new 1954 aqua and white two-tone Ford Fairlane parked in the driveway. He stopped and looked back at Vivian who was watching him from the front door.

"Don't forget the dry cleaning and give them that dress. It needs taking in."

She mechanically touched the dress as she watched him open the door to the car.

"Paul," she shouted, "Happy…"

"It looks like rain," he stated, cutting her off as he got into the car and slammed the door shut.

"Yes. Yes it does," she whispered as she watched him back out of the drive.

She waved to him, still clutching the wrapped box and then looked up to the beautiful, sunny, cloudless sky, and frowned.

TWO

BOA CONSTRICTORS

Vivian changed into a simple blue button-down shirt-dress minus the belt. It hit her leg about mid-calf and had large sensible patch pockets. It was quite stylish with its capped three-quarter length sleeves but without the cinching at the waist, she looked like she was wearing her grandfather's nightshirt.

She slipped into a pair of sensible flats and checked herself briefly in the bathroom mirror. It's not that Vivian was unattractive; she just didn't know how to play up her best features. Her self-cut shoulder length hair needed a style and what make-up she did wear, just wasn't the right choice for her pale skin tone. She studied the woman looking back at her in the mirror and sadly realized that she hadn't a clue.

Still thrown and depressed at how the celebratory breakfast played out, or didn't, she glanced at her wristwatch and walked out of the bathroom as if she were on automatic pilot. She picked up her uniform from the bedroom floor and headed downstairs. She passed through the kitchen, which she hadn't bothered to clean up, grabbed her purse and left through the front door.

It was unseasonably warm for early September. In fact, the summer of 1954 in Abbot was a scorcher, breaking all temperature records. What rain they did have evaporated as quickly as it fell.

With a glazed look on her face, Vivian came out of her house, locked the front door and headed to the garage. Paul promised that when they married he would take care of the gardening but obviously he hadn't stayed true to his word. The rhododendrons, azaleas, evergreens, and juniper bushes that bordered the 1930s cape had long since withered and died. And the front lawn was so parched, what was grass now looked like a yard full of hay. The extreme heat had even made the red paint on the siding of the house chip and peel, which to Vivian, made it look like it had chicken pox.

She had to use all her strength to pull up the warped wooden windowless garage door. There sat her dusty 1944 second-hand Buick sedan. She jerked open the rusty door and climbed up into the driver's seat. After a few tries she managed to start the engine. Without looking behind her, she backed out and swiped the car against the side of the garage. She had no reaction.

Oblivious to the world, she continued down and out of the drive and onto the street. Without checking for traffic, she just missed hitting another car as it passed by the house. The driver honked their horn, startling Vivian, as she ground the gears into first and drove on.

The Hayes lived on Osgood Street, which was peppered with beautiful homes and manicured lawns. Considering her upbringing, it was ironic that Vivian's house was definitely the eyesore of the neighborhood.

As she turned off of Osgood and onto Clark Road she passed by two women walking arm-in-arm. Over the years she had trained herself not to look, but she could tell from her peripheral vision that the moment they sited her driving by in her boat-sized jalopy, their two heads turned to each other so quickly they looked like magnetic kissing dolls.

The town of Abbot was small and quaint but the residents were bored and nosey. And the gossiper's favorite target was the poor little rich...poor girl. The townsfolk had a morbid curiosity about Vivian, as if they delighted in knowing that this child that was born into so much luxury, money and prosperity, was now living such an austere and peculiar life.

Most thought Vivian had skin as thick as an elephant because she never seemed to be fazed by the townsfolk talking about her. Intellectually she wrote it off as small town mentality. But as a coping mechanism she developed the unhealthy ability to put blinders on, and shoved each little jab, snicker and rumor farther and farther down inside of her. In truth, each whisper felt like a tiny dagger stabbing her in the back. And those who didn't talk behind her back pitied her, which hurt her even more.

Clark Road began at the top of a hill and was famous for the number of eighteenth century colonial homes that were built along it. The first and most splendid mansion was called the Shepherd house. As a small child Vivian was occasionally allowed to visit a young playmate that lived there but only if she were accompanied by Maid 4. More interested in the house than the child she was playing with, Vivian sensed there was something about that property and its land that always felt safe and enveloping to her.

Each magnificent house that led down to the Drake River had on top of it a widow's walk. Sea captains built them so their wives would have better views of their ships as they returned home from long voyages. The Drake River was large enough and Abbot just 22 miles from the Atlantic Ocean, that vessels could make their way inland along this route. In winter months, if one glanced back up the hill through the leafless trees, it looked like stadium seating as each estate rose higher than the next, stretching to get a better view of the fast and furious river.

Vivian sailed down Clark Road in her own boat till she eventually reached River Road at the bottom. No trains were coming and the rail guards were up so she clunked over the Boston and Maine tracks then crossed the Drake over the wrought iron arch bridge. To her right was the slow, drought plagued river and to the left were her father's abandoned, four-story high brick mills.

She turned left onto Mill Street and chugged up the steep incline as if she were riding a cog railroad. Once at the top, she passed the glaringly white South Church and coasted into the center of town.

Normally for Vivian, driving by the Abbot Movie House and checking to see if the marquee had changed was like a child eagerly running to the mailbox waiting for a much-anticipated letter. But deep in thought she hadn't even noticed that they had switched out the sign.

THE COUNTRY GIRL
starring **GRACE KELLY** and **BING CROSBY**

Coming Next

A STAR IS BORN
starring **JUDY GARLAND** and **JAMES MASON**

And as she approached the first intersection in town she slowly ran the red light on Main and Essex Streets. Luckily, out of the corner of her eye, Vivian saw Nancy Hodges pushing her daughter Jenna across the street in her baby stroller. She slammed on the brakes and just missed hitting them.

"Jesus Christ, Vivian!" Nancy hollered. "We have the light!"

Vivian rolled down her window. "Nancy, I'm so sorry."

She watched as Nancy shot her a dirty look and then pushed her daughter safely to the other side. Exhausted, Vivian rested her forehead on the giant steering wheel of the Buick. Within moments the light changed and a car behind her blared its horn.

After three tries, she managed to shift the car into first and drove on.

With her car parked out in front of the Abbot Village Dry Cleaners and taking up two parking spaces, one could vaguely see Vivian through the dusty front window. She stood on a box as a seamstress worked on her uniform.

"Turn please, Mrs. Hayes," she mumbled with a mouthful of pins.

Vivian turned and stared blankly over the woman's head and at the newspaper her husband was reading at the counter. The front-page headline screamed:

I LOVE LUCY RATED
TOP TELEVISION SHOW
Even President Eisenhower does not want
to be disturbed while show is on the air.

Robotic-like, Vivian came out of the cleaners weighted down with a box of shirts, several pairs of pants on hangers and one of Paul's uniforms. She opened the passenger's door, threw the clothes onto the seat and then checked her watch. She heaved the heavy door shut and then rushed to get into the car.

As Vivian pulled out of the dry cleaners and tore down Main Street heading for the town library, one could see she had caught one of Paul's pant legs in the door and was dragging it along the road.

~ ~ ~

"Our next garden tour will raise money for The Home For Little Wanderers," Gloria Goodson declared with great pride. "Ladies, I think you'll agree with me that these orphans need all the support we can give them."

The large circle of women, seated facing each other in the

community room of the public library, nodded in agreement.

Gloria looked over at Vivian whose face was buried in a legal pad of notes. "Vivian, can you read the minutes from last month's meeting?"

The gals all looked over at her as she hung her head low.

Gloria cleared her throat trying to get her attention. "Viv?"

Sitting next to Vivian and hard to miss was Babs Parker. She had her long wavy copper red hair conservatively pulled back in a ponytail. She was wearing skintight pedal pusher pants with large red roses printed all over them and a man's crisply ironed white dress shirt tucked in, with the collar up. If the womenfolk of Abbot viewed Vivian as the social outcast, then they saw Babs as the renegade risk taker.

In the same class at school, Babs and Vivian certainly made for the odd couple. The popular kids shunned them both hence they bonded quickly. Babs was fascinated by Vivian's eccentricities, Vivian mesmerized by Babs' sense of humor. Vivian had a boyish figure and on occasion was actually mistaken for a man from behind when wearing pants. Babs was all woman. She had voluptuous hips accentuated by a tiny waist and with a 37-inch chest; she could fill a bra and was proud of it. The big challenge for her was that she had grown into this very womanly figure at the mere age of 11.

Nicknamed Frick and Frack by schoolmates, they were each other's only friends, hence by default, best friends. But as open and free as Babs was, Vivian still protected herself emotionally behind an impenetrable wall, even with Babs.

Gloria tried once more. "Vivian!"

Still oblivious to the calls, Babs kicked Vivian's foot with her wedge sandal, which sent the notebook sitting on her lap flying onto the floor.

"Looks like rain!" Vivian blurted out.

Confused, the group of women looked at each other and then towards the sun pouring in through the oversized library fan windows. Embarrassed, Vivian scrambled to pick up her papers.

"A weather girl you'll never make," Babs whispered as she knelt down to help her.

"Ladies?" Gloria said standing up. "I think we're done for the day. And don't forget the bake sale next Saturday afternoon at West Parish Church."

Frazzled, Vivian turned to Babs as they all started to leave. "You free for lunch?"

"Sure kid," she said as they filed out behind a very stunning and younger woman. "Viv, I've never seen you so wound up."

"I'm fine, really. I'm...fine." She gestured to the girl. "A new member?"

"Eleanor Gates," Babs whispered.

Dressed inappropriately in a strapless cocktail dress and with an extra long mink stole scarf draped over her arm, she worked her way out of the library as if it were a high fashion Paris runway.

Vivian leaned to the side and caught a better glimpse of her face. "Kinda looks like Ava Gardner."

"Oh please, no one looks like Ava."

"Is she a horticulturist?"

Babs elbowed Vivian. "You got the first syllable right."

Vivian's jaw dropped. "Babs!"

"Delores Gilmore told me the only thing she's done in a garden is get deflowered."

Vivian couldn't help but smile. "Shhh. She looks harmless. But a stole in this weather?"

Eleanor raised her voice so all the other women could hear her as she spoke to another member. "Look what I got out of him," she purred as she stroked the mink.

"Do I hear wedding bells?"

Eleanor stopped and looked at her. "His wife can keep him, I'll take the gifts." They both cackled as Eleanor swung the end of the stole around her neck almost hitting Vivian in the face.

Babs pulled Vivian back. "As harmless as a boa constrictor."

There was a pause and then they both broke out into laughter as they left the library.

~ ~ ~

For 1:30 P.M. on a weekday, DeQuatro's Italian restaurant was unusually busy. Although some patrons were starting to leave, the bar was still packed and a fog of cigarette smoke hovered over the sea of red and white checkered tablecloths.

A waiter stopped at the girl's table and cleared away their plates. Babs had finished everything on hers; Vivian hadn't touched a bite. He tried to take Vivian's almost empty martini glass but she grabbed it away from him.

Babs continued with her dating tales of woe. "So I met this guy and after a couple of dates he invited me back to his charming double-wide trailer for a night cap and he says he's going to change into something more comfortable." Babs looked around and lowered her voice. "And when he reappears he's dressed in nothing but a corselette girdle and stockings."

With no reaction, Vivian took out a cigarette.

"A girdle!" Babs repeated dramatically.

Vivian lit up, took a long drag and blew the smoke out the corner of her mouth.

Babs shook her head. "You haven't listened to a word I've said."

"So, you bought a girdle." Vivian downed the last of her drink and signaled the waiter for another.

"Is this a liquid lunch?"

"Just a little thirsty today." Vivian nervously picked at the candle wax that dripped down the straw covered Chianti bottle sitting between them on the table.

Babs looked at her watch, grabbed her handbag and then gestured to a movie magazine stuffed into it. "I'm just scratching to see *The Seven Year Itch*, aren't you Viv?"

"No."

"The buzz is Marilyn kills."

"She isn't relevant. No one takes her seriously."

"I think every man would take her…seriously. And a few women too."

That actually made Vivian laugh.

"So Viv, will you come to one of my parties?"

"Money's tight."

"Forget about buying anything, I need bodies. You might win something."

"A fly swatter?"

"Or a gravy boat."

Vivian snickered. "My gravy could sink a boat."

"Sales are so great, Stew is now working with me part-time."

Vivian laughed harder. "Your brother the cop is a Tupperware lady?"

"I'm selling, he's handling the inventory."

Vivian looked at her watch as the waiter placed her martini on the table. She chugged half of it. "I'm late for a doctor's appointment." She downed the rest of the drink and sucked hard on her cigarette.

"Another test?"

Vivian got up and opened her purse. "I really think I am this time."

Babs stood and placed her hand on Vivian's. "Put that away. Lunch is on me. And happy anniversary, Viv," she said as she embraced her.

"Glad someone remembered." Vivian dug her cigarette out into the ashtray. "Call me madcap but I'm still insanely in love with the man."

"Insane you are, Madcap. As long as you're happy." Babs put money on the table and they both walked towards the exit.

Vivian didn't respond.

Babs touched her arm. "You are happy, aren't you?"

"Deliriously," Vivian said a little too enthusiastically. "Paul's just distracted with work and under a lot of pressure at the station."

"Well, if that's all it is. I'm gonna touch up my face and rush to a party over on Elm."

Babs watched as Vivian took a step towards the door and noticed a woman across the room who was smoking, drinking and eight months pregnant. She paused briefly, looking at her enviously.

Babs came up from behind and brought her lips up to Vivian's ear. "It'll happen one day." She kissed her on the cheek. Vivian smiled at her and left the restaurant as Babs headed for the ladies room.

Moments later, Babs re-emerged having applied a fresh layer of Max Factor's Ruby Red lipstick then headed to the front bar and lounge. She glanced up at a giant advertisement as the bartender came over to her.

Your voice of wisdom says **SMOKE KENT**

Babs shrugged her shoulders. "I guess it's a pack of Kents, please."

She dug into her purse for money when she heard a woman laugh at the far end of the massive oak bar. A policeman sat very close to her with his back to Babs, hiding the woman's face.

"Thirty cents, Ma'am," the bartender said as he put the cigarettes on the counter.

Babs looked back up at the sign. "My voice of wisdom says I'm getting ripped off." She opened the pack, took out a cigarette and the bartender lit it for her. She took an exaggerated drag and blew it into his face. "And it's Mademoiselle." She stepped away.

"Yes, Ma'am."

Babs did a double take and then the woman at the end of the

bar laughed even louder. Babs took her glasses out of her purse and slowly walked down to the far side of the lounge trying to get a good look at the couple.

The woman laughed again seductively as she and the cop huddled together. "Show me another," she cooed.

Babs worked her way through the maze of patrons drinking at tables as she moved closer but all she could see were the man's hands. He slipped a cigarette into his left fist, lit end first.

"Oh no!" squealed the woman.

He squeezed his hand and she gasped. He squeezed it harder and smoke drifted upwards. Suddenly he opened his fist, the cigarette was extinguished and his hand had not suffered.

His female friend applauded. "How did you do it?"

"I need my reward first," the policeman said.

"As long as you have more tricks up your sleeve."

They separated as the woman got up off her barstool and that's when Babs' jaw dropped. Eleanor Gates sat upon Paul Hayes' lap and kissed him passionately.

Babs' hands flew to her mouth. *Paul's under pressure? I'd say about a 110 pounds worth.* She grabbed the large cocktail menu off of a table and hid her face behind it while Paul and Eleanor continued to kiss, oblivious to the world.

Babs rushed back to the front of the bar, threw the menu down and made a beeline for the exit.

"Thank you, Ma'am," the bartender said.

"Mademoiselle!" she shouted as she left.

Outside of the restaurant Babs ran to her lime green second hand Ford sedan. She eyed the backseat, which was full of Tupperware products and then checked her wristwatch. She knew Vivian's doctor's office was on the west side of town but the Tupperware party was on the complete opposite. She jumped into her car and paused for a moment having to make a decision. She shifted into forward and took a fast right out of the parking lot.

THREE

LEFTOVERS

Vivian sat nervously opposite three very pregnant women in her gynecologist's waiting room. The doctor was extremely behind in schedule.

"My husband just looks at me and I get pregnant," said the one heaviest with child of the three.

Vivian picked up that week's copy of *Life Magazine* featuring Judy Garland on the cover as Vicki Lester in the movie *A Star Is Born*.

The second woman rubbed her swollen belly and laughed. "I think it's something in the water."

Vivian pulled the magazine up in front of her face and flipped through pages pretending to be fascinated by the ads for low riding Studebakers, Blue Bonnet Margarine and Audrey Meadows endorsing O'Brien's Liquid Velvet wall paint.

The third spoke up and declared, "Whoever said cheaper by the dozen oughta be shot! I'm getting my tubes tied after this one."

Suddenly the room was quiet. Vivian peeked out over the top of the magazine and all three were staring at her. She gently touched her non-existent baby bump.

"Um, this is my first."

The nurse entered, rescuing Vivian. "Doctor Moody will see you now, Mrs. Hayes."

~ ~ ~

As Vivian zipped up her dress in the doctor's examining room she noticed a poster advertising condensed milk. A young woman was happily bottle-feeding her newborn child as the ad explained:

Why slow down your busy life breastfeeding
when baby can be artificially fed?

Evaporated canned milk with corn syrup and limewater.

CONDENSED MILK makes mother's and baby's life
HAPPIER and HEALTHIER!

Vivian found the baby's face familiar and then remembered the first doll her father had given to her as a young child. Unfortunately, it was a short life, for the doll that is. The moment Vivian's mother discovered it she had Maid 1 toss it away.

But knowing of his daughter's love of dolls and trying to quell his guilt over spending more time at the mills than he was at home, Mr. Lawson secretly supplied his daughter with an over abundance of them. Vivian hid them in an almost inaccessible eave in the attic over the Maid's quarters. And only when her mother was dining at the club or out for a game of tennis and the Maids weren't in their rooms, would Vivian run up to the attic and play with the dolls, doting over them for as long as she could.

She was obsessed with the need to mother and she knew why. Vivian's intense desire to have children and shower them with love was her attempt to heal her own personal wounds and offer a child what she never had, tenderness and nurturing.

Nervous at how long it was taking for Doctor Moody to return, Vivian started to pick away at a hangnail. She studied the poster for artificial feeding and decided it wouldn't be the right route for her. The doctor finally entered the room reading Vivian's chart and coughing while a cigarette dangled from his lips.

"The test results came back, Vivian."

"Did the rabbit die?" she asked sarcastically.

His dangerously long ash fell ominously onto the examining table. "I'm afraid not."

"But Doctor, I haven't had my period and I'm like clockwork."

He held out his pack of cigarettes offering one to her. She shook her head, but he insisted. "It will calm your nerves."

She pulled one out and he lit it for her.

"Vivian, the records indicate you've lost more weight. Have you been eating?"

"Well, not yet today but…"

"Hmmm."

"What does 'hmmm' mean?"

"The problem may not be you. We need to check your husband's sperm count."

Vivian frowned. "How do you do that? With a blood test?"

Doctor Moody actually chuckled. "No dear, he…supplies us with a…sample."

She took a puff of her cigarette and then realized what he was alluding to. "Oh, um, no. I don't think he…ah, that's not an option."

"Go home. Talk to him." Dr. Moody then took a small bottle out of the medicine cabinet. "You need to relax Vivian if you want to get pregnant. When jittery, take one of these."

She looked at him, worried.

"Trust me," he said as another ash toppled from his cigarette and landed on his potbelly.

~ ~ ~

Babs regretted her decision to go to the Tupperware party instead of running over to Doctor Moody's. Still at the gathering, she took a quick moment to call Vivian from the kitchen of the hostess's home in hopes that she could reach her. She frantically dialed her number while the women out in the living room chirped away.

"Burp it again!" shouted one guest.

Babs looked back towards them nervously. "Pick up, Viv. Pick up." She let it ring a few more times and then hung up the phone.

"Sit on it!" screamed another woman from the living room.

There was a moment and then Babs registered what the woman had said. She made a frightened face and ran out of the kitchen.

~ ~ ~

Later that afternoon Vivian stood before a small three-pound prime rib sitting in a roasting pan on top of the Wedgewood. Intimidated, she studied her opened cookbook once again. "Preheat oven to 500." She looked at the dial on the oven. "Hmm, it only goes to 450." She looked back at the recipe. "Roast for 15 minutes then reduce to 325 and cook 15 to 17 minutes per pound for medium rare." Vivian gulped. Math was never her strong suit.

She glanced up at the wall clock and realized it was just after four. She guessed Paul should be home by 5:30 P.M., which would give the roast plenty of time to be done and for them to enjoy a drink and some hors d'oeuvres before they had dinner. She tentatively opened the oven, shoved the roast in and slammed the door shut as if the meat was going to jump back out at her. Having accomplished that much she wiped her hands together like she had won this round, poured a glass of wine and headed upstairs.

Vivian was certain that the anniversary dinner she was surprising Paul with was going to make-up for the disastrous break-fast. She walked into her bedroom and fumbled, unbuttoning her dress. She held out one hand and noticed it shaking. *I think this qualifies as jittery.*

She grabbed her handbag and pulled out Doctor Moody's bottle of pills. Vivian entered the bathroom, popped one into her mouth and washed it down with the wine. And with a little extra time on her hands, she drew herself a well-deserved bubble bath.

~ ~ ~

Out to the world, it was Vivian's own snore that woke her up in the tub. Surprised that she hadn't drowned, she managed to get out of the now chilly bath feeling as though she had consumed the entire bottle of wine.

"What the hell was in that pill?"

She grabbed the bottle and all it said on it was:

*   Moody   *

Vivian wrapped herself in a towel and sat down at her vanity. She focused on her face but was literally seeing double. She picked up an eyebrow pencil and although her hands were no longer shaking, they also weren't obeying her commands. She drew a thin brown line, trying to arch it over her left eye but it was like the hand had a life of its own and it veered off towards her ear.

"Damn."

She smudged the end off and tried doing the right brow but this time her arched line went up a little too high creating a surprised look. She smeared some brownish eye shadow onto her lids and then tried her best with black eyeliner and mascara. Vivian quickly rouged her cheeks, applied a layer of red lipstick and then took a breath. She gazed into the mirror and what stared back at her looked like a startled circus raccoon.

Suddenly she perked up and sniffed the air.

"Oh no," she slurred. "The roast!" She could smell it burning.

She stumbled out of the bathroom in her towel and grabbed the staircase railing for support as she almost tripped running down it.

Vivian spun around into the kitchen and discovered it was engulfed in smoke. She opened the oven door causing more to billow out into her face. Coughing, she turned off the Wedgewood, grabbed two potholders, dragged the roast out of the oven and threw it up onto the top of the stove.

"Darn it!"

Still wrapped in just a towel and barefoot she picked up the charred beyond recognition smoldering pan of meat and carried it to the back kitchen door and hip checked it open. She managed to slip through but the door slammed shut behind her.

Vivian felt water, stopped and looked up to the sky. "So *now* it decides to rain?"

The droplets made the roast sizzle and pop in the hot pan as she ran over to the trashcan. She kicked it knocking the lid off and dumped the roast in. Just faintly she could hear the phone ringing in the house as the light rain began to pour.

"Shoot!"

She ran to the back door and tried to open it but it had self-locked behind her. Vivian dropped the pan, tightened the towel around her body and then scurried down the drive to the front of the house.

"Ow, ooh, eeh, ouch!" she cried as she stepped on pebbles and stones.

She flew around the corner of the house, up the cracked cement walkway, which had now turned into a river of water and dirt and grabbed the front doorknob. She turned it and nothing happened. She grasped onto it harder, turned it again and butted her shoulder into the door and still, it didn't budge.

"Damn it!"

The heavens opened up and the rain became torrential. To the right of the front door was a solid picture window, but to the left, the dining room window had two, pane over pane sliders. She stood on her tippy-toes and strained to open the first one but it was locked. She tried the second one and it too was locked. Just then a car drove by the house and when its headlights hit Vivian, she spun around as if she were in a police lineup and screamed.

Desperate to get into the house, she ran back along the drive and noticed the kitchen window above the sink was ajar but too high for her to reach. She made her way over to the side of the garage and dragged back a huge wooden ladder. At this point her feet and legs were covered in mud as the kitchen phone continued to ring.

Vivian lifted one end of the ladder and banged it up against the house next to the window. She wiped her soaked and stringy hair away from her face and climbed the rungs. She managed to push the small window open wider, grabbed onto the sill and shimmied her body in.

Inside, she had to worm her way across the sink of dirty dishes, pots and pans but her towel was caught on the ladder. She fell to the floor stark naked with the phone still ringing.

"Ahhh," she squealed.

Vivian got to her feet and grabbed a potholder to cover her crotch and then realized how ridiculous that was considering she was completely alone in the house. She threw it down as the phone rang once more. She ran to the kitchen extension and picked it up.

"Hello?" she answered completely out of breath. "Hello!"

All she heard was a dial tone. She dropped the receiver and slid down the kitchen wall next to the open oven. Exhausted, scraped and bruised, naked and drugged, and with her make-up running, Vivian looked like a second rate Hollywood starlet starring in a B-horror movie called *The Wedgewood*.

~ ~ ~

Across town, Stew Parker was waiting in his squad car for Babs. A bit nerdy and out of shape, he was the complete antithesis of the stereotypical policeman. A year and a half older than his sister, most mistook Stew for being Babs' little brother. Not so much because he looked younger, it was more about the dynamics of their relationship. She was mothering, demonstrative and constantly giving Stew advice. He was always second-guessing himself, and in truth, felt overshadowed by her self-confidence and more often than not, acquiesced to her many whims. He followed her around like a tickbird to a rhino. And like the bird and mammal's symbiotic relationship, Babs may have been the fearless and larger than life character, but Stew was the alarm system, ready to sound off noisily when danger approached. It was a good match.

Wearing black horn-rimmed glasses with lenses that needed to be strengthened, Stew brought his wristwatch up to his face to read the time. Wondering what was taking Babs so long, he impatiently followed the windshield wipers back and forth as they laboriously worked to slosh away the rain.

Babs ran out of her house with a Tupperware bowl over her head and opened the passenger's door.

"Hope this storm doesn't put a damper on the party turnout," she shouted as she climbed into the squad car and threw the bowl into the backseat.

Stew rolled down his window so he could actually see if any other cars were coming, then he pulled out into the street. "I'm late for my shift."

"Sorry for holding you up. Having trouble reaching Viv."

A serious look came over his face.

Babs continued. "If I didn't have these two parties back-to-back I would have swung by her place."

"Anything wrong?"

Babs shook her head now regretting that she had brought it up. She never could keep a secret and cursed herself as she nonchalantly looked out of the fogged up window.

There was a long pause and then he hit his fist on the steering wheel. "Not again."

Stew was an emotional man who tended to wield his hands wildly when excited, in an expressive way, but not threatening.

"Listen, don't get in the middle…"

"Who is it this time?"

Stew knew exactly what was going on. In fact, everyone at the precinct knew of Paul's philandering ways. Some of the guys on the force found it amusing, even impressive. But Stew had morals and principles and would have found his behavior disgusting no matter whom Paul was married to. But because it was Vivian, it pushed every reaction button Stew had in his body.

Babs debated whether or not to tell him, then blurted it out. "Eleanor Gates."

Stew slammed on the brakes bringing the cruiser to a screeching halt causing Babs and the entire backseat full of Tupperware to lurch forward. A plastic tub came flying forward into the front seat as a car passed by them blaring their horn.

Babs touched his hand gently. "Stew, please don't…"

He was seething. "I'm finally going to confront the heel."

"But don't do anything crazy." Babs picked up the container and threw it into the backseat as Stew just sat there fuming. She glanced at her watch and gently reminded him of the time. "Um, we're both really late."

Stew turned on the car's siren and tore off down the road blinded by his anger and the rain, with his hands flying.

"Oh geez," Babs cried as she and the Tupperware felt the force of his car press against them.

~ ~ ~

After consuming copious amounts of water to counter the effect of the mystery Moody pill, followed by several cups of black coffee, Vivian managed to set the dining room table. Because she and Paul eloped, she had no bridal shower, therefore received no gifts. Not even from her mother. But there was someone who knew of her secret wedding and once she had settled into her house, sent over a brown paper wrapped boxed with a note attached that simply read:

good luck,
maid 4

Inside was a beautiful Irish lace tablecloth with bright red trim that she had crocheted herself. Maid 1 and Maid 3 were already ancient when Vivian was born and had no real relationship with her at all. And it was clear that Maid 2 disliked Vivian chatting at her because inevitably she would end up burning herself with the iron. But unlike the others, Maid 4 did speak to Vivian but only when they were on outings like to the Shepherd house. And although they never had true conversations and most of Maid 4's orders consisted of "Hurry up!" or "Watch your step!" and "Don't be late!" Vivian interpreted her deep Irish brogue barking as kind and protective words of wisdom.

Vivian had lovingly spread the lace tablecloth out over the dining room table. She then laid out two settings of her multi-color Melmac plastic dinnerware and matching hand-blown goblets, pairing them up with vintage silverware she had picked up at a garage sale. She gathered several candlesticks from around the house and had timed lighting the candles to coincide with Paul's arrival.

~ ~ ~

Hours later, Vivian stood in the doorway of the dining room and looked at the candles that had burnt down and out. Paul had ordered her never to call him at work but worried that something serious had happened, either a robbery or a shooting, she wondered if she should dial the precinct.

Working the front desk, Stew had his head buried in a phone book while fellow Officer Pete O'Reilly sifted through a pile of papers.

"Stew, maybe she spells it G-A-Y-T-E-S?"

He shook his head. "I think the problem is, she's just too new for the system."

Stew took off his hat revealing a premature friar's tuck. The perfectly round balding pattern on the back of his head looked like a child's beanie cap had worn it away. As a policeman, what he lacked in projecting authority and brawniness, he made up for with fairness and compassion. And as much as he tried to hide it, the torch he was carrying for Vivian was blazing bright and strong. He was determined to catch Paul in the act and save Vivian from anymore heartache.

Pete got up and went to a file cabinet. "Maybe she moved here in time for the latest census."

The phone rang and Stew answered it in a forced, gruff voice. "Precinct Four, Officer Parker."

Vivian was on the other end. "Stewie?"

His voice softened. "Oh, um, hi Viv."

"Can I speak to Paul please?"

"Paul?"

She half-laughed. "Yes, my husband?"

Stew panicked. "Aw, gee, Vivian. He's ah, not here right now. He had an emergency."

"Oh no," she said clearly upset. "I knew something was terribly wrong."

"No, he himself didn't have an emergency. There was a call and he, well, um, he had to go to the scene of an emergency."

Vivian paused, trying to take this all in. "Are you all right?"

Officer Pete came up beside Stew. "Gates, I found it." Stew quickly covered the phone's receiver.

"Stew, did someone say Gates?"

"Um, no, Viv. Cakes." Stew turned his head away from the phone knowing how stupid that sounded. "It's a couple of the guy's birthdays this week and we're celebrating and Pete found the cakes."

"Oh, OK. Stew, I'm sorry for bothering you…"

"Not at all."

"But I always get nervous when Paul's late and doesn't call. And I'd never check up on him unless it was important but tonight is our wedding anniversary and…"

This really fired Stew up. "Not to worry, Viv. Sit tight. You have no idea how sorry I am that you're having to go through all of this."

Vivian looked puzzled, trying to decipher what he was referring to. "OK."

Stew caught himself and tried to cover. "I promise you he'll be back before you know it."

"Thank you." Confused, Vivian slowly hung up the phone.

Stew put down the receiver as Pete came over. "She's at 12 Morton Street."

"Cover the desk," Stew said as he ran out of the station.

~ ~ ~

The rain had just ended as Stew's police car pulled up in front of Eleanor's house. He got out of the cruiser and walked past Paul's Fairlane parked in her driveway. He paused for a moment actually trying to figure out what he was going to do and say. Stew took a deep breath but held it, causing his chest to puff out as he walked up to the front door and rang the bell.

He waited a moment, exhaled and rang the doorbell again. Getting no response, he knocked on the door. Then, he knocked harder. Infuriated, Stew slipped his billy club out of its holder and banged it against the door.

Finally it opened. There stood Eleanor barely wrapped in a pink chenille bathrobe and her black mane of hair tousled.

She smiled at him nervously. "Yes, Officer?"

Stew used his gruff voice. "Tell Paul Hayes to come to the door."

"Who?"

"Cut the dumb blonde..." Stew paused realizing her hair was black. "Just tell the moron to come to the door."

Paul appeared at the door in just his boxers.

"What the...?"

Stew puffed his chest up again. "Go home to your wife."

Paul pushed Eleanor to the side and filled up the doorway. "Who the hell are you to tell me what to do?"

Making sure he kept his distance, Stew pointed his finger repeatedly at Paul as if he were digging it into his chest. "It's your goddamn anniversary for Christ's sake."

Stew turned away in disgust and walked back towards his car.

"Oh that's right, judge me and then run for cover."

Stew kept walking, holding his breath and trying to look larger than he was while sweat poured from his armpits.

"Come back here, you sissy. OK. That's it. Just keep walking. You're going to regret you ever did this Parker!"

Stew hopped into his car and with a shaking hand managed to get the keys into the ignition wondering if the brute was going to chase after him.

He finally released his breath, deflated his chest and sped off.

Paul screamed at the top of his lungs, "Asshole!"

~ ~ ~

Vivian stared blankly at the tail end of the Miss America pageant. She tugged at the hangnail she had prepped in Dr. Moody's office as Bob Russell, the host, stood between the last four contestants. The television was flickering and scrolling and with a touch of the rabbit ears, she could have stabilized it, but her mind was elsewhere. Her eyes focused on the coffee table where the small wrapped present sat.

Was there an emergency? Maybe Paul was hurt. She pinched the hangnail between her thumb and index finger and knew she shouldn't do it. *There was obviously something Stewie wasn't telling me. Why was he fumbling so? Maybe Paul was with another…*and she ripped the skin off of her finger.

There was a moment before the pain registered in her brain and then blood began to drip. "Oh geez."

Cupping her hand, she went into the kitchen and wrapped it in a napkin. After blotting some blood away she examined it. *Congrats Vivian. Tore this one down to the first knuckle.*

The pain she understood, the waiting was driving her mad. About to jump out of the rest of her skin, she went back into the living room.

Bob Russell continued with the television show. "We're down to our last two ladies but first we'd like to thank you, our television audience for tuning in to the first nationally televised broadcast of the Miss America pageant." There was tremendous applause from the audience and a quick shot of the judging panel, which included Grace Kelly. "The two very excited and nervous gals standing beside me are Miss California, Lee Ann Meriwether and Miss Florida, Ann Gloria Daniel. And the winner is…"

Vivian turned off the television set. She walked over to the picture window and pulled the curtain aside, looking out. There was no sign of him. She tightened the napkin around her finger and was tempted to call the station again but decided not to.

She paced the living room floor and that's when she heard his car pull into the drive. Caught off guard, her first reaction was to run to the door. She thought twice about it and went into the kitchen, dabbed her finger one more time and threw away the napkin. Determined not to look as though she was waiting for him, she scurried over to the sofa, sat back down and picked up a copy of Anaïs Nin's *A Spy In The House Of Love*. She flipped open to the dog-eared page and heard his keys in the door. She fought her instinct to jump to her feet and then took a deep breath.

Paul entered and was momentarily surprised that the dining room table was so elaborately set.

"Oh, you're home," Vivian said, sounding as nonchalant as possible. She casually got up off of the divan walked over to him. "Happy anniversary, darling." She stretched up to kiss him but he gave her a peck on her forehead.

Trying not to react, she strolled into the kitchen. "Go, sit. Get comfortable. I'll bring you a beer." She took a bottle of Rheingold out of the refrigerator. "I was going to serve a roast but I'm afraid there was an incident and I've reheated last night's dinner." She took a casserole dish out of the oven and placed it on the dining room table. "I picked up your dry cleaning and had my dress altered." She went back into the kitchen and popped the top off of the bottle of beer.

Vivian walked casually into the living room with the beer but Paul was gone.

"Paul?"

She actually ran to the front window to see if his car was still there, and it was. Thinking he must have gone upstairs, she grabbed the gift from the coffee table, put it in her pocket and went up with the beer.

"Paul?" she asked again as she reached the top of the stairs and stood in the doorway to their bedroom.

Paul came out of their bathroom wearing just his boxers. Vivian paused admiring his body. He had massive shoulders that narrowed down to his waist. His arms were strong and vascular, his legs powerful and defined. And he had the perfect amount of body hair, which highlighted his muscles making it look as though an artist had painted them on. Once on a trip to the Boston Museum of Fine Art, Vivian stood before a breathtakingly beautiful Greek statue and realized that was Paul's body. She found it both intoxicating and irresistible.

She snapped out of it and handed him the beer. "Oh, I saw Doctor Moody today and well, it was a false alarm. But I'm sure next month I'll do much better and oh…" She took the gift out of her pocket. "It's nothing too fancy but I thought you'd like it."

Surprisingly, Paul pulled her close to him. "Let me give you my gift first."

He brought his lips close to hers and then paused a moment. The hesitation made her dizzy with anticipation. He slowly planted his full lips onto hers and kissed her deeply.

But as Paul unzipped her dress allowing it to fall to the floor, the phone started to ring. Not knowing what she should do, Vivian just stood there in her bra and half-slip. She was about to speak but he put his finger to her lips. He literally swept her off her feet into his arms and carried her to the bed, laid her down and kissed her again even more passionately.

Paul's gift slipped from her hands to the floor as he ravaged her from head to toe, except for touching the scar around the waist. He never did and never would. It wasn't out of respect for Vivian's self-consciousness about it. It was because it repulsed him so and Vivian knew it.

On this rare and erotic occasion, he pulled out all the stops knowing exactly how to pleasure his wife. Vivian's need for Paul's affection was like a parched and wilted flower thirsty for rain. She was in heaven. Time stood still and the world was good again.

~ ~ ~

Sated, Vivian laid on her stomach wrapped in the sheets with her head turned away from the bathroom. She had dozed off and now half-conscious, she wondered if what she had experienced really happened or if it was just another dream. She heard him in the bathroom and closed her eyes. Although exhausted, the thought of him making love to her again made her feel exhilarated.

Paul came out of the bathroom completely dressed and sat next to her on the bed.

"Vivian?"

She kept her eyes closed and smiled coyly as she wrapped her arms around his waist.

He paused. "Vivian, I'm leaving you."

Her eyes instantly opened wide. Paul attempted to move but Vivian's grasp tightened around him.

"Vivian."

He tried to stand up.

"Let go."

Paul tried prying her arms away but she clenched harder.

"Vivian!"

He escaped from her grip and walked over to a packed suitcase sitting by the bedroom door. Totally thrown, she sat upright trying to collect her thoughts. Without looking at her he left the room.

She jumped to her feet, grabbed her bathrobe and ran out after him.

Paul had reached the bottom of the stairs and stopped, keeping his back to her. "Vivian, your hair's a mess, you're a terrible cook and you're barren." He turned and walked away as she flew down the stairs. He passed through the dining room to get to the front door as she appeared.

"Any husband in his right mind would leave you. You're like, you're like cold..." and without even giving her the decency of looking her straight in the eye, he just casually gestured to the dining room table, "...leftovers."

Then, something absolutely extraordinary happened. Vivian spoke back.

"You bastard," she whispered viciously.

Paul came to a complete stop. "What was that?" he asked incredulously. And before he could turn around to look at her, she was on top of his back.

"You goddamn bastard!" she screamed at the top of her lungs as she locked her forearms around his throat and her legs around his waist forcing him to drop the suitcase. She squeezed as hard as she could, marveling at her own strength. Never did she think she could feel so much rage.

Neither did Paul. Unable to breathe, let alone speak, he stumbled into the living room squirming to get her off of his back. But she was up for the fight. The adrenaline pumping through Vivian's body signaled to her that she could hang on all night if she had to.

"Who?" she demanded.

Squeezing his throat even tighter, Paul choked. "Ugh... awww...eeeeh..."

"Tell me!"

He managed to get out, "Who...what?"

"Who the hell is the other woman?" Vivian couldn't believe the power she felt. It was both thrilling and frightening at the same moment. If need be, she thought she could crush him. "Who is she?" she screamed louder than she ever had in her life.

"El..."

Paul whipped around thinking he could fling her off but Vivian wasn't budging.

"What's her name?" she shrieked, almost demonically.

For a split second she eased up on his thorax and he spit it out. "Eleanor Gates."

Vivian let go of her grip and slid down his entire body till she hit the floor.

"Eleanor Gates?" she whispered.

Paul rubbed his throat and coughed. "You know her?"

Vivian started laughing hysterically. "You idiot. She's already got some fool wrapped around her little finger buying her mink stoles."

"I bought her that."

Very slowly, Vivian got up to her feet as Paul cautiously watched her.

"Were you just with her?" she asked, in a frighteningly calm voice.

He looked down at the floor. She took a step towards him and he hung his head lower. And then it happened. With 25 years worth of unexpressed wrath surfacing from her belly, Vivian made a fist, pulled her arm back and with all her might she threw an uppercut punch that slammed up into his chin. Having caught Paul's tongue between his teeth, blood squirted everywhere.

He felt his mouth. "You cut my tongue!" he muttered through the spit and blood.

She threatened him. "I'll cut more than your tongue, you bastard!"

"Bitch!" he slurred.

"Oh, you think this is being a bitch?" Vivian ran to the fireplace mantel and grabbed a framed picture of the two of them. She spun around and threw it at him just missing his head. It smashed against the wall shattering glass everywhere. "How long? One week? Two weeks? A month?"

"Five months," he stated, almost proudly.

Like a tornado, Vivian went ballistic ripping the room apart. Anything and everything that wasn't bolted down she started hurling at him: a vase, an ashtray, a book, even a floor lamp.

"Why?" she demanded as she picked up a glass paperweight from the desk.

"Why what?"

She threw the weight, which he tried to dodge but it got him right in the solar plexus. He doubled over trying to catch his breath.

"Why did you just…make love to me?"

"I thought it was the decent thing to do," he admitted, sheepishly.

This sent her over the edge. She started pummeling him with magazines, pillows, a waste paper basket and another lamp.

Protecting his face from the flying objects Paul shouted out, "I love Eleanor!"

"You don't know how to love anybody but yourself!"

He cowered as she threw more things at him forcing him towards the front door.

"And Eleanor loves me!"

Vivian ran into the dining room and picked up a candlestick. "She's a whore," she screamed as she threw it at him. It just missed his head, embedding itself into the wall.

"Vivian?" Paul said as his picked up his suitcase. "This is really unattractive."

She looked at the table as he opened the front door. "Leftovers are never pretty!" she screamed as she lifted the casserole.

Paul flew out of the house just as she heaved the leaden Pyrex dish at him like a shot put. It sailed out of the house and smashed onto the concrete walkway.

Vivian ran to the front door as Paul made a getaway in his car. She screamed at the top of her lungs, "And the doctor said it's your fault!"

~ ~ ~

Vivian stood in the shower for over half an hour aggressively scrubbing her skin with soap trying to get Paul off of her. She looked at her right hand and examined the reddened knuckles that were beginning to swell. Shaking, she turned off the water and grabbed a towel.

Drying herself off, she walked into the bedroom. On the floor was Paul's gift. She picked it up, looked at it for a moment and then surprised herself by caressing it gently. She looked over at the framed picture of Paul on her night table and picked that up too.

She touched his face. The anger and strength that Vivian had felt was liberating and empowering but terrifying at the same time. As quickly as it surfaced, she tried desperately to push it down, feeling guilty about what she had just done. Vivian may not have needed a professional to help her realize why she so passionately wanted children, but she certainly could have used a therapist to help her deal with the sick and dysfunctional relationship she had, not only with Paul, but with her mother as well. But her generation frowned upon psychoanalysis and the townsfolk of Abbot already had plenty enough to talk about. She didn't need to add mental illness to the list.

As Vivian's rage dissipated, utter sadness crept in and that's when the floodgates opened up. She gathered Paul's picture and gift into her arms and collapsed onto the bed sobbing uncontrollably.

The phone started to ring again but she paid no attention.

FOUR

THANKS FOR GIVING

As quickly as Vivian allowed her protective walls to come tumbling down, she rebuilt new ones that were twice as large and even more impenetrable. It was her survival technique.

A few weeks after he left, Paul sent Vivian a letter from a lawyer explaining that he wanted the easiest and fastest divorce possible. Hence, he flew down to Juárez, Mexico for a "quickie". Only one partner in the marriage needed to apply making these proceedings very attractive to estranged American couples. The Mexicans called it a "divocios al vapor". Translated, it basically meant – divorce granted as rapidly as marriage evaporated. All Paul had to do was go to the city hall, pay a fee and the divorce was final in about three hours.

If that wasn't humiliating enough, Vivian was mortified when she discovered that Eleanor went with him and the travel agency they used offered a package deal, which included: legal representation, round trip airfare, transportation, room and board, plus a cocktail.

Once the marriage was over, Vivian became more and more

reclusive. No longer did she participate in the Garden Club or any of the other, few, social activities she was involved in. The only person who seemed concerned about her was Babs. But Vivian shut her out too and stopped answering phone calls all together.

Days blurred into weeks and Vivian only left her house when she needed essential items. Food was rarely high on the list. A huge pile of mail had accumulated in an unused wooden salad bowl that sat in the middle of the kitchen table. All bills, Vivian never opened them. She had but a small amount of cash on her; therefore when she did venture out for purchases, she charged everything to store credit.

On one such rare occasion, she threw on her uniform, covered her head in a scarf and headed out the back kitchen door. A brisk and sunny autumn afternoon, Vivian slipped on a large pair of dark sunglasses, climbed up into the Buick and managed to start her up on the fifth try. She backed it out of the drive and put it into park, as she checked the mail.

When she opened the box a flood of bills and collection notices spilled out onto the sidewalk. She gathered up the envelopes, stuffed some into her purse, threw the rest into the back of the car and then pulled herself back into the driver's seat. She revved the engine, shifted into first gear and the car's exhaust system back-fired. A bright orange flame leapt out of the muffler as the car burped out a loud pop and then stalled. Unfazed, Vivian shifted into neutral, started it again and took off down Osgood Street wearing her blank, public face.

She turned the corner onto Clark Road passing by the Shepherd estate. Its ancient maple tree on the corner of the property was blazing with orange and red leaves proudly displaying its fall foliage but Vivian didn't notice.

She sailed down the hill. The oaks, beeches, dogwoods, and hickories all screamed at her to admire their color but Vivian was in her own world. When she reached River Road, she plopped over the railroad crossing, drove over the roaring Drake River via the wrought iron bridge, turned left and chugged up Mill Road.

With South Church on her left Vivian reached the crest of the hill and then coasted into the center of town. She passed by the Abbot Movie House oblivious to the marquee, which now advertised:

A STAR IS BORN
starring **JUDY GARLAND** and **JAMES MASON**

Coming Next

WHITE CHRISTMAS
starring **BING CROSBY** and **ROSEMARY CLOONEY**

She traveled down to the west end of Main Street where Sutherland's Department Store was located and tried to park the Buick in no more than two parking spaces.

Inside, she grabbed a shopping cart and slowly walked up and down the aisles of the expansive store. She picked up various inexpensive items such as toothpaste and shampoo. Several light bulbs had blown out pitching lamps at Paul and she was just now getting around to replacing them. And in the clothing section, she chose a gray cable knit cardigan. She slipped it on and although it was a size too big, she tossed it into her basket. The furnace had been acting up, shutting off when it shouldn't be, and the house was getting cold so she picked up a simple blanket to keep her warm on the sofa at night and worked her way to Claire, the cashier.

"Good afternoon, Mrs. Hayes," she said as she started ringing up the items.

Vivian looked up at her. "It's Lawson. Miss Lawson now."

Claire glanced at the wedding band she was still wearing, causing Vivian to slip her hand quickly into her pocket.

"But Claire, we've known each other for years. Please call me

Vivian."

Claire smiled. "Will this be cash or store credit?"

"Credit please," Vivian said as she glanced out of the large department store window.

It was then that she noticed the golden afternoon sunlight flickering through the vibrant leaves of an elm tree standing guard out on the sidewalk. The site reminded Vivian of an impressionistic painting and for a brief moment she thought this is what her life had become; painted by someone else and out of focus.

The cashier coughed to get her attention.

Vivian turned back around. "Claire, it's a beautiful day, isn't it?" she asked tentatively, suggesting that she needed her agreement to make it true.

Instead of listening, Claire was studying a clipboard. "It says in our records that you have reached your credit limit."

Vivian looked at her innocently. "What does that mean?"

"That you have to pay cash."

"But why? I haven't purchased anything here in ages."

Claire's finger traveled down a long column of numbers. "Well, the last item listed here is a pricey mink stole."

Flustered and embarrassed, Vivian turned to make an escape out the front door.

"Enjoy the beautiful day, Mrs. Hayes."

Vivian left the car where it was parked and walked aimlessly down Main Street. As she passed the Abbot Bookstore and then the Town Florist's shop she wondered how many other stores Paul had maxed out their accounts at. Worried about what to do, she drifted down Acorn Street and paused realizing she had stopped in front of Paul's father's barbershop.

She quickly turned around and made a right onto Main. There stood the Abbot Savings Bank and she hurried in.

~ ~ ~

Vivian sat opposite Henry Laytner, a very old and tidy banker. Growing impatient trying to read his face, she studied his desk. Every item was set perfectly in its place. Pens were all facing the same way, papers were piled in crisp stacks, even his phone sat perfectly angled with the corner of the desk. As he continued to scour endless account pages, Vivian looked out the bank's window and realized the sun was setting on her impressionistic painting. She had to break the silence.

"But Henry, I have money of my own."

He continued to examine the numbers. "You also had a joint account." He shuffled a few more pages, put them down and looked at her seriously. "And it's empty."

Vivian wasn't sure if she heard him correctly. "There's nothing left? At all?"

He closed her file. "You have $135.25 in the checking account."

"But the savings?"

Sympathetically, Henry shook his head.

Vivian was stunned. "But...but isn't there something where I can take a loan out against my house?"

He stood up. "You could but you're months behind in mortgage payments. I'm telling you right now, you won't qualify."

Vivian looked as though she were about to cry.

"You could try suing him but it's obvious he has no money either."

Sick to her stomach, Vivian stood up. "Thank you, Henry," she said almost inaudibly. She started to walk away and then turned back to him. "This is a little embarrassing. Paul...obviously took care of all the finances and well...could you show me how to write a check?"

Henry smiled warmly as Vivian sat back down. She opened up her purse to take out her checkbook when a few of the bills fell to the floor. As she picked them up she looked at one. "And what would happen if say, I didn't pay the electric bill for several months?"

"They'd turn the power off."

"Oh my."

After Henry showed her the correct and very tidy way to write out a check, Vivian left the bank and stood out on the sidewalk wondering what she should do. She saw Aquarius Hardware across the street and got an idea. Without looking, she stepped out into Main Street and almost got hit by a car. They honked their horn as Vivian stepped back up onto the curb and once the light turned in her favor, she ran across the street and into the store.

Moments later she came back out looking dejected. She walked further along on Main till she reached Gloria's Bakeshop. She hesitated for a moment and then entered.

Beyond charming, Gloria had gingham curtains hanging in the windows and French café tables and chairs set up inside. Anyone walking into the shop and smelling the delicious confectionaries baking inside would always feel like they've stepped back in time into Grandma's kitchen. Well, anyone but Vivian.

She walked up to a young girl working behind the counter. "Excuse me, Miss."

She looked up at Vivian and then over to the clock on the wall. "I'm sorry, but we're closing."

Vivian tried to see past her into the kitchen. "Is Gloria here?"

The girl nodded, stepped into the back room and Gloria appeared covered in flour.

"Viv," she exclaimed as she came out from behind the counter and they hugged. "It's so good to see you. We've missed you at the Club."

"I've been a bit…"

"Honey, I understand. You know I've been through the big "D" myself. But are you taking good care of yourself? You look awfully thin."

Vivian pulled her to the side. "Gloria, I'm really strapped. I was wondering if you needed another girl to work the counter."

"Honestly, I don't. But I could use a baker."

"Only hire me if you want to kill your customers."

They both laughed.

"Oh Viv, I've missed your sense of humor."

"Who's being funny?"

"Say, have you tried Aquarius Hardware?"

"They just hired a girl."

"Is there anything else you can do?"

"You know I'm not the best secretary."

They embraced again. "Dear, if I hear of anything, I'll give you a call."

When they separated Gloria noticed Vivian eyeing the sticky buns in the display case. She thought quickly and ran around the counter, tossed the rolls into a box and handed them to her.

"Oh Gloria, I can't..."

"It's closing time. I'd have to throw them out anyway."

Vivian graciously took the box from her, blew her a kiss and then awkwardly left the shop.

Gloria watched her leave while shaking her head.

Vivian walked back to the Buick parked at Sutherland's. She threw the buns into the car and hauled herself in. With it getting darker she turned on the car's headlights as she pulled out onto Main Street but instead of going home her usual route Vivian turned right instead of left.

Main turned into Route 1 as she continued to drive north, frantically thinking of what to do. Without realizing it she had crossed over into the neighboring town of Norwich.

She passed by Coleson's Tree Farm and Nursery and laughed. *I've killed every plant I've ever owned.*

She traveled on going by the Reid Plastics Corporation and then saw the bright orange roof of the Howard Johnson's restaurant and shook her head. *I don't think being a HoJo waitress is in my cards.*

About a half mile down the road she came upon the enormous

blinking neon sign for the slightly seedy-looking motel, the Shalimar. But with four of the letters not working, the remaining ones screamed out:

S H A L I M A R

Vivian pulled the car into the motor court and parked in front of a room as a middle-aged chambermaid came out with a cigarette clamped between her lips. She pushed her cart to the next unit.

"Excuse me, Miss," Vivian shouted as she climbed out of the Buick. The chambermaid turned quickly and looked at Vivian suspiciously as she came over to her. "Can I ask you a few questions?"

The maid nervously looked both ways to see if anyone was watching. "You're not with the police too, are you?"

"Oh no."

The woman looked Vivian up and down. "You write for a travel guide and you're rating us?"

"I'm afraid not. I was thinking of applying for a job. Do you enjoy your work?"

She laughed cynically. "Do I enjoy scrubbing toilets full of some stranger's deadly germs and changing sheets stained with God knows what? Do I enjoy risking my life every day not knowing if some pervert is about to jump out of a closet and kill me? Do I enjoy working for minimum wage?" She paused for a moment. "I guess so."

"How much is minimum wage?"

With a disgusted look on her face, she took one last drag of her cigarette, tossed it onto the pavement and ground it out with her shoe. "Seventy-five cents an hour."

"That's all?"

The chambermaid leaned in to Vivian. "Don't tell the boss but once in a while a guy will tip me five, sometimes ten bucks to tuck him in real tight at night. And I'm not talking hospital corners."

Vivian responded naively, "Oh?" She repeated to herself what the maid had just said. "Oh." Then, Vivian got it. "Oh!"

She rushed to her car, hopped in and sped down Route 1 back to Abbot.

~ ~ ~

A few weeks passed by and Vivian's salad bowl of bills and late notices grew so large they spilled out onto the kitchen table. There was also an annoying notice someone kept putting up on her front door, but knowing that whatever it was it wasn't something she could take care of, she just kept tearing them up and throwing them away. Running out of time and money, she realized she had to do something she had sworn she'd never do again in her life.

She drove the Buick, which was making a strange scraping sound underneath its belly, into Manning's Service Station on the west side of town and parked it in front of a pump. The car gave out one large belch before the engine shut down. A young man came out and around to Vivian's window as she rolled it down.

"Hey Johnny."

He rubbed his hands together. "Gettin' pretty cold, isn't Mrs. Hayes?"

"It's Miss..." She shook her head deciding it wasn't worth trying to change her name. She opened her purse and started digging around.

"Your car sounded kinda strange comin' in." He walked around it. "They say we might have snow on the holiday."

Vivian counted any nickels, dimes and pennies she could find. "What holiday?"

He came back around to her side and laughed. "You're so funny, Mrs. Hayes."

She looked at him blankly.

"Thursday? It's Thanksgivin'?"

"Oh, of course." She made it sound like an oversight but truthfully, she had totally forgotten. She momentarily thought of the impressionistic painting, realizing each day was blurring into the next.

Johnny kneeled down and took a look under her car. "Mrs. Hayes, looks like your muffler is draggin' on the ground."

"Oh really?"

"You oughta get that fixed before you lose it."

"I can't afford..." She paused and decided to rephrase her remark. "I can't afford the time. I have to make it into the city and back. Just give me a dollar's worth of gas?"

"Sure thing."

~ ~ ~

As Vivian scraped and clunked her way down Route 1 to Boston she had to think hard to remember the last time she had seen her mother. She visited Irene as seldom as possible. Both mother and daughter preferred it that way. But when money was involved, Irene had made it clear early on that it would never happen over the phone. Vivian would have to ask for it in person, face-to-face. She knew it was because her mother enjoyed watching her squirm.

Irene now lived in an historic row house in the affluent neighborhood of Beacon Hill in Boston. The Abbot mansion proved to be too much property for her. She had plenty of money for the upkeep but it was just too cavernous and full of unpleasant memories for her. Plus, the number of household staff had dwindled.

Shortly before Vivian married Paul and after decades of pushing and pulling a heavy iron back and forth over Irene's wrinkled belongings, Maid 2 was forced to retire due to rheumatoid arthritis. Irene tried to bribe her to come back against her doctor's orders, and she wanted to, but sadly the bones in her right shoulder were so fused it's as if the joint had been soldered together making it one solid piece of stone.

The next year, Maid 1 was waxing the kitchen floor and complained of a sore back. Irene reluctantly allowed her one day off to rest and the situation became worse. The next day an ambulance arrived at the house and took her to Bon Secours Hospital in the neighboring town of Lawrence where she had every test done imaginable. The following day and before any of the results had a chance to come back, she died. An autopsy revealed that her spine was riddled with cancer. Vivian had often thought she was the most stoic of all the maids. But not to feel, or maybe to hide the symptoms of a growing cancer like that, was quite remarkable.

Less than a year later, a 4 foot 11 inch Maid 3 was tipping the scales at 220 pounds. Although Irene ate like a bird and preferred a diet primarily consisting of vegetables and grilled fish, Maid 3 had a passion for fried foods. Anything and everything that she could fry, she did. On one occasion Vivian walked in on her deep-frying batter dipped bacon. So it was no surprise that on one Saturday night while devouring a second helping of southern fried chicken plus a dozen fried hush puppies and downing it all with two large glasses of buttermilk, her heart exploded killing her instantly where she was most comfortable, in the kitchen. It was just Maid 4 and Irene left.

Irene put the estate, which William had built for her, up for sale. It boasted seven bedrooms with seven attached baths, two formal living rooms, one formal dining room, one casual one off of the solarium for breakfast and lunch, a library, a billiards room, a sewing room, four maid's rooms, two maid's baths, a professional kitchen and eight fireplaces. It also had five acres of land, a guest cottage, a tennis court and an Olympic size swimming pool. In 1952 when the average cost of a house was $9,050 the Lawson's mansion sold for a whopping $849,250.

The row house Irene purchased on Beacon Hill was situated on Pinckney Street. The gaslit cobblestone lane proudly displayed one exquisite brick house followed by another, each adorned with brass knockers and intricate ironwork.

Irene's house was rumored to be haunted by its former tenants: Louisa May Alcott, Henry David Thoreau and Henry James. And, although not part of the famous literary scene, now Irene Lawson was bound to add her own peculiar ghost to the list. The four bedroom, four bath house that Irene and Maid 4 moved into was practical, except for its narrow footprint. Space had to go up, rather than out and the amount of stairs proved challenging for both women.

Once Irene moved into the city she realized how plebian it was to be living up in Abbot. Now she had the opportunity to go to the theater, opera, concerts and museums whenever she wished. Not that she necessarily had an interest in the arts, Irene just wanted to be seen. She dove into the social scene head first starting off with joining the very exclusive Banam Club. A combination private restaurant and meeting ground for the very elite, the stately property was situated on Beacon Street facing Boston Common, just three walking blocks from Irene's house.

~ ~ ~

As Vivian passed through Everett and approached Chelsea just outside of Boston, she encountered a sea of potholes on the highway. Trying to dodge the pockmarks, she narrowly missed hitting another automobile but managed to catch the back tire of the Buick in a giant crater. Instantly the car's muffler was ripped off and went flying off the edge of the highway. Frightened to stop on the shoulder, Vivian continued on her way into the city driving what sounded like, an out of control rocket engine.

She crossed the Mystic River Bridge and once in Boston she managed to get herself over to the Charles River. Following it south she wormed her way down to Beacon Street and then hoped to find an on-street parking space. To her amazement she found one almost in front of the Banam Club. While only hitting the car in front and in back of her three times trying to parallel park the car, she very noisily squeezed herself into the spot. Vivian waited for the delayed snapping and popping to quit as the engine shut down, then checked herself in the rearview mirror.

Vivian kicked open her door and slid out of the Buick wearing a threadbare beige raincoat spotted with stains. She stood outside the Club, which was located in an historic townhouse, took a deep breath and then climbed the steep steps up to the front door.

She wasn't sure if she was supposed to knock or ring the bell, so she just opened the door herself. Upon entering there was a spiral staircase leading up to the next floor and tucked under the case was a woman playing a harp. The walls of the foyer were a dark rich paneling and the floor, an imported black and white marble.

Clearly annoyed that she let herself in, a maître d' dressed in tails and white gloves quickly approached Vivian.

He looked her up and down, gave her a displeasing glare and then raised his hawk-like nose high into the air. "May I help you, Madam?"

Totally out of her element, Vivian tried to disguise the tremor in her voice. "I'm meeting Irene Lawson."

"You mean Mrs. William Lawson?"

His pretentiousness cured her of her self-consciousness. "No," she said with attitude, "I mean my mother."

Another butler type character appeared and surprised Vivian by trying to take off her raincoat. She resisted at first but then realized she was going to have to surrender it. After a firm tug, he pulled it off her and there she stood in what she thought was her best outfit. Unfortunately, it was also a summer dress. Another hand me down from Babs, the loose fitting white cotton dress with bright orange floral print would have been perfect for an afternoon lunch by the pool but looked shockingly out of place in this stuffy supper club towards the end of November.

With great reservations the maître d' stepped into the opulent salon to the left and gestured to Irene. "Mrs. William Lawson," he said to Vivian as his upper lip curled, disapprovingly.

Vivian took a deep breath, held her chin high, threw her shoulders back and walked into the Banam dining room.

There she was, sitting at a table for two beside the roaring fireplace. Irene was holding a newspaper up in front of her face.

Impeccably dressed in a two-piece magenta tweed Chanel suit, she wore a diamond necklace and had her brunette hair neatly pulled up and back in a casual bun. In the spring she had had very successful plastic surgery shaving years off of her life. Now she could have easily passed for a woman in her late forties. But no matter how hard she worked on her outward appearance, what she was clearly lacking was inner beauty.

Vivian tentatively walked over to her table and waited to be acknowledged. After an extraordinary amount of time had passed, she stepped towards her and gave Irene a quick peck on the cheek as she continued to read the paper.

"Hello Mother."

Vivian pulled out her own chair while glancing over at the judgmental maître d' and sat down.

Without moving the paper, Irene spoke. "Reichold Chemical is up 32 percent. Did you buy their stock when I told you to? Today it's plastics, plastics, plastics."

"Hello to you too, Vivian," she whispered to herself.

Irene put the paper down. "I don't get a kiss?"

Vivian rolled her eyes, got up, walked over to her mother, kissed her dispassionately on the cheek again and then sat back down.

Irene studied her. "What in God's name are you wearing? A summer frock just before Thanksgiving?"

Vivian fumbled. "My other dresses were at the cleaners."

Her mother looked at her suspiciously "Hmmm. What warrants this unexpected request? The last three times were about money."

"Maybe I just wanted to have lunch."

"Maybe you should wax your upper lip."

Shocked, Vivian's hand flew to her mouth as Irene signaled to the waiter.

"And have a professional show you how to draw those nonexistent brows on. What did you use, a crayon? You look like a man."

The waiter appeared as Vivian dropped her head.

Irene gestured to Vivian. "My daughter will have a drink."

Vivian looked up at him rather anxiously. "A vodka marti…"

Irene cut her off. "Seltzer with a dash of bitters. And I'll have another side car."

The waiter bowed and left the table.

Irene looked at her silverware and wiped a spot off of her knife with her napkin. "How's Peter?"

"Paul."

"Same thing."

"Paul and I…"

"I still don't know why you ever married that man, not that beggars can be choosers."

Vivian took a deep breath. "We loved each other."

Irene guffawed in her face. "He loved your father's money."

"I'm sure you did too." Vivian couldn't believe what flew out of her mouth.

"I beg your pardon? I may not have gone to school but I invested every penny your father ever made and tripled his fortune. Technically, I made more money than he did."

Vivian realized she had to get to the point, then get out of there as fast as possible. "Mother, I need to ask you…"

"I need to ask you again, when are there going to be grandchildren? I want to be young enough to enjoy them."

The question, to Vivian, seemed so absurd. Irene couldn't stand the sight of her, why would she want her kids?

"Mother, maybe you should have had more than one child."

"More? It's not like your birth was planned. It was 1929 and we were in a depression."

"The country was, you weren't."

Irene huffed. "I had to be practical. I'm a very pragmatic woman."

"Yes you are," Vivian said under her breath.

"Why are you being so impertinent today?"

There was a long pause as they both looked awkwardly around the room.

Irene fiddled with her pearl necklace. "What does Peter do nowadays?"

"He and I…"

"Honestly, child," she said cutting her off once again. "You always bring things back to you. I, I, I, me, me, me. It sounds so selfish."

Vivian took another deep breath. "I don't care what Paul does. I need to ask you if I can borr…"

"You don't know what your husband's doing? Vivian, how cavalier. You're lucky I set you up with the money I did after your father died. Spend it frugally and invest it well because you're not getting another dime from me."

Vivian bolted out of her chair and towards the door.

"Vivian? Vivian!"

The waiter arrived with the sidecar and seltzer.

Irene leaned around him to look at her daughter. "How rude." She glanced up to the waiter. "When my daughter returns tell her I'm dining alone."

The waiter nodded and left the table as she took a large swig of her drink and picked up her newspaper. "That'll teach her."

Vivian darted out into the foyer, startling the maître d'.

He pointed to the left. "Ladies lounge to the left."

"I want my coat."

"With pleasure."

He retrieved it and held it out to her like he was going to contract a disease. She grabbed it from him and escaped out the front door, slamming it behind her. Amazed at her own fury, she had to hold onto the black wrought iron railing to steady herself as she walked down the steps to the street. She could have lashed out at her mother. She could have killed her mother. But she wouldn't have gotten what she needed. As she made her way to the Buick wondering what she was going to do, it started to snow.

~ ~ ~

And it continued to do so, very heavily, during the drive back to Abbot. The only good thing about Vivian's tank was its weight. Any other automobile, without snow tires or chains, would have skidded off of Route 1 and become stranded just outside of Boston. But Vivian's Buick skied smooth and steady back to her house. Snow was drifting from north to south so she was even able to yank open the garage door and get it into the shed and out of the elements.

As freakish as the late summer's extreme drought and heat wave was, it didn't compare to the amount of snow that was dumped on this small New England town. It continued to snow up to and through Thanksgiving.

That morning Abbot looked like the quintessential picture postcard. Like royal icing used for gingerbread houses, gobs of snow clung to bare tree branches, piled high on windowsills of every building, and even made South Church's steeple seem that much closer to heaven. And quiet. The blanket of snow created a deafening hush throughout the village.

As the day began, golden lights twinkled from homes here and there, as curls of smoke drifted up from chimneys into the sky and families began preparing for the day's celebration.

Exhausted, Vivian slept late. Normally she would have showered and gotten dressed but she wondered what the point would be. All she had for breakfast was black coffee and just after 11:00 A.M. she turned on the television. She had no interest in watching the Macy's Thanksgiving Day Parade, but the sound of it felt comforting. With no plans, she stretched out on the sofa, pulled a blanket up over her head and fell asleep.

Hours later it was the roar of the crowd at the Missouri versus Maryland football game on television that woke Vivian up. Actually hungry, she went into the kitchen and stood in the middle of the room, dazed. In her cupboards were some cleaning items along with baking soda, baking powder and a few dried spices. She opened the refrigerator revealing condiments like ketchup, mustard and relish. A jar of pickles sat in a green sea of mold and a head of lettuce was beginning to decompose in the crisper. On the counter was a set of canisters. She opened each one as if she had no idea what was in them. Flour, sugar, salt and surprisingly, the fourth one had some white rice in it. She threw it into a pot with some water and lit the Wedgewood without any fear at all. In fact, she dared it to blow up.

Forty-five minutes later the sun was beginning to set while it continued to snow. Vivian sat at her kitchen table looking at the pile of bills as she tried to scrape undercooked stuck rice off of the bottom of the pan. She picked up one envelope, which indicated it was from the electric company and threw it back onto the table. She tried to eat another spoonful of rice and all of a sudden, the lights went out. The power was cut off and the football fans cheering on television dissolved into a moan and then dissipated to nothing.

Not surprised, not angry, not anything, Vivian just sat there in the dark.

~ ~ ~

No more than an hour later and still snowing, Babs carefully drove down Osgood Street with chains attached to the back tires of her car. Stew sat in the passenger's seat with a tower of Tupperware full of food on his lap.

"Babs, when's the last time you saw her?"

She thought hard. "I don't remember."

"Why did you stop calling?"

"Stew, I stopped calling because Vivian was never home."

"Or she never picked up."

As Babs pulled up in front of the house she strained to see out of the snow-covered window. "I don't see a single light on."

"Maybe she went to her mother's for the holiday?"

"God help her if she did."

Babs got out of the car and slid her way around to Stew's side as he opened his door. He started to get out and she pushed him back in. "Are you crazy? You'll do more damage to your foot." She took the Tupperware containers from him as he fought with his crutch and then shut the door.

The snow was knee deep as Babs plodded her way towards Vivian's house. Slowly, she carved out a path to the front door. Completely out of breath, she rang the doorbell, but there was no sound. She tried ringing it again and then knocked on the door. Getting no response, she dug out a spot in the snow with her hands and put the food-filled Tupperware down into it and then backtracked down the walkway and worked her way to the garage.

So much snow had fallen since Vivian had parked the Buick that Babs couldn't see any tire tracks. And with the garage door windowless, she couldn't tell if her car was in there or not. She made her way to the kitchen door and pounded on it.

"Viv!" she hollered. "Vivian, are you in there?"

Still getting no response and beginning to shiver, Babs tried scraping off the ice that had accumulated on the back door window but she couldn't see in. Her thighs started to burn as she trudged back to the car.

She opened her door and fell onto the driver's seat. "I don't think she's there," she said breathlessly. "No answer and can't tell if the car's in the garage."

"What did you do with the food?"

"Dug a hole and left it on the front step."

Stew shrugged his shoulders as Babs closed her door and shifted into first. "This snow isn't going anywhere fast," he said. "Wherever she is, the food will still be fresh and frozen till she gets to it."

They both laughed nervously as she drove off.

In total darkness, Vivian sat at the kitchen table almost comatose. She was emotionally spent and nutritionally deprived. If only Babs could have seen in through the window, she might have noticed the red glow of Vivian's cigarette as she took another drag.

FIVE

CHUBBY BUNNIES

The next day it finally stopped snowing. It was sunny and cold and like all true-blooded Yankees, the townsfolk of Abbot quickly banded together clearing the streets and sidewalks preparing for one of their busiest shopping days of the year.

Vivian had fallen asleep on the sofa and eventually woke up when she heard some sort of drilling coming from the front of the house. She got to her feet and feeling a bit dizzy, staggered to the door. She opened it and found to her surprise, Henry Laytner standing there, watching Carl Willows trying to remove the lock from the door.

"Vivian," Henry exclaimed, as he looked very tidy with his pant legs tucked into his galoshes. "You *are* home."

"Yes," she replied.

"We knocked for a long time," Carl said, as if he was caught doing something wrong.

"Vivian, this is Carl Willows."

Carl turned to Henry. "Viv and I went to school together."

"Yes, we did."

There was an awkward pause and then Henry cleared his throat. "Vivian, I'm so sorry, but we have to change the locks."

She looked at him, confused.

"The bank posted several eviction notices on your house," he continued as she looked at him vacantly. "You must have seen them."

"I suppose so."

"You had a couple of weeks to move your belongings out. The bank now owns the house."

"Oh my."

There was another awkward pause and Henry cleared his throat again. "Uh, we have to ask you to leave."

"OK," she said unemotionally as she gestured for them to come in.

At first sight, both Henry and Carl were taken aback at how the living room looked. Vivian had never picked up the objects she had thrown at Paul back in September, nor had she cleaned or straightened up the place. Newspapers, magazines, dirty glasses and dishes littered the room.

Henry took out the handkerchief from his suit's breast pocket and dabbed it to his nose. "Vivian, the bank will hold your possessions for a period of time and you'll be able to reclaim them but..."

She cut him off as she headed upstairs. "There isn't anything I want. I'll pack a suitcase and come back down."

~ ~ ~

Carl was kind enough to shovel the drive so Vivian could back out of the garage with the Buick.

And Henry felt horrible about having to throw Vivian out of her house. "You're going to be OK, Vivian?" he asked as he helped her into the car. "You have some place to go?"

"Yes Henry, I'm fine."

She shut the door and vicariously backed out of her driveway in her muffler-less jalopy and out onto Osgood Street. Worried, Henry watched her as Carl posted the foreclosure notice on the front of the house. She stripped the gears shifting into first, headed towards town and never looked back. As she rumbled on, the corners of her mouth curled up slightly as she envisioned all the unpleasant memories she had experienced while living in that house, finally being locked up for good.

She turned right onto Clark Road and passed by the estates, each trying to outdo one another with opulent fall wreaths mounted to their front doors. Reaching the bottom of the hill, she turned right onto River Road and bumped over the railroad tracks, crossing the snow covered Drake River via the wrought iron bridge. She then turned left onto Mill Road and inched her way up the incline, leaning forward trying to help the Buick as it made it to the top. She passed South Church on her left and then coasted towards town. Everything looked so pristine and magical, as if all were covered in marshmallow and ice. Anyone else would have thought they had fallen into a Currier & Ives winter wonderland print, but not Vivian. Like a flame that was just about to burn out, she suddenly had a burst of energy and clarity, and had only one thing on her mind.

Instead of driving by the Abbot Movie House, Vivian took a right onto Central Street for two blocks and stopped at the corner of Lowell Junction. The Buick was definitely on its last legs but valiantly got her to her destination, Axelrod's Used Cars.

Vivian turned into the lot and before she had a chance to park the wreck, it spitted and sputtered and after releasing a tremendous backfire, it died. Wearing a pair of ankle high boots and with her raincoat over her uniform, she eased herself out of the Buick and stepped into a deep slush puddle. Numb already, she hardly felt the ice water burning her feet. She reached into the car and dragged out her one suitcase and headed over to the office.

Vivian leaned on a 1953 Thunderbird convertible parked in

front of the dealership as Bill Axelrod came out to greet her.

"Good day, Vivian." His first reaction was that she seemed to be rather underdressed for the weather.

"Hey Bill."

"What can I do you for?"

She held onto the Thunderbird and tried to get the water out of her shoes.

Bill stroked the car lovingly. "Gorgeous."

"What?" Vivian asked looking up at him. For a moment she thought he meant her. "Oh yes, yes she is."

There was a long awkward pause as Bill searched for something to say. "Ah, looking to buy another car, Vivian?"

"Actually, I was wondering what you could give me for the Buick."

"Let's see." Together they walked over to the car. "It's a 44? Makes it 10 years old. Would've cost you about $750. Beauty in its day." He walked around it. "You got some pretty good dings in it. Missing a taillight. Did someone hit you from behind?"

She nodded as he unsuccessfully tried to open the trunk. He walked around to the other side, which was dented and severely scraped from Vivian scratching her way out of the garage. Bill opened the passenger's door and noticed the leather seat was torn. He leaned in and looked at the speedometer.

"A lot of miles you've put on it," he said shaking his head as he got out of the car and shut the door. "Sorry Vivian."

"Please Bill."

"Just keep driving it till it stops."

"I did."

"It's really not worth…"

"I'll take anything for it."

"Sorry," he repeated, apologetically.

Vivian followed him back to the office and then noticed a sign hanging in the window.

SALESMAN
WANTED!

"Wait! You want a new salesperson?"

"You mean Paul?"

"No, you didn't hear? He and I split up. Bill, I'm flat broke. And I lost the house."

"Foreclosure?"

She got very excited. "If you hire me, I'd work really hard and I think I could..."

He cut her off, laughing. "Oh Vivian, we don't let women sell cars." He looked at her face and then realized how desperate she was and changed his tune. "Maybe I can use the Buick for scrap?"

"But Bill, if you give me a chance."

"Will $25 help?"

Dejected, she nodded as he counted out the money from his pocket and handed it to her.

"Thank you." She picked up her suitcase.

"Can I give you a lift somewhere?"

"No," she said barely audible. "I'll walk."

Vivian turned and headed towards town, sloshing through snow and puddles as Bill went back into the office. With no sidewalks on either side of the road, she lugged her suitcase down Lowell Junction for three blocks to Main Street as cars sped by spraying snow and ice water. Not quite sure what she should do, Vivian headed to Gloria's Bakeshop. At the very least, she could get a hot cup of coffee and try to dry out her shoes.

The sidewalks on Main were clear and full of shoppers eager to take advantage of the holiday bargains hence no one noticed Vivian as she made her way with the heavy valise. Tired, cold and hungry, she stopped in front of Gloria's to catch her breath. When she turned to enter the café she saw, sitting in the front window at a table for two, Eleanor and Paul holding hands. Embarrassed, Vivian hid her face and scurried away.

Feeling beaten down and hopeless, Vivian walked and walked and walked. Not paying attention to where she was going and shivering to the bone, she found herself surprisingly at the bottom of Mill Road. Instinctively, maybe she was walking back towards the house, but as she went out onto the wrought iron bridge she stopped mid-way.

She looked out into the river and saw that the sun, shining warm and brightly, had melted a small hole in the ice and she could see the rushing water below. She put down her suitcase and stepped up onto it. She paused for a brief moment and then swung one leg over the railing, and then the other. Vivian sat there looking out at the mill her father had built as thoughts and images flashed through her brain like a strobe light. Snapshots of her mother, her dolls, the Shepherd house, her father's funeral, Maid 4 and Paul. Her eyes welled up with tears as she leaned forward to jump.

At that exact same moment, Babs was crossing the train tracks in her car with Stew, a trapped listener in the passenger's seat. The look on his face indicated clearly that she had been on another roll about another date.

"Actually he was a blind date, Stew, set up by a friend. Well, I thought she was a friend. This guy was so obnoxiously full of himself. You know, a real bragomanic."

Babs laughed hysterically as Vivian, out on the railing, had a split-second of clarity. *What in God's name am I doing?*

She swung her legs back towards the bridge to safety just as Babs and Stew passed her. Simultaneously, both their heads spun back to look at her.

"Is that Vivian?" Stew hollered out as Babs slammed on her brakes and laid on the horn.

Startled, Vivian looked up, lost her balance and fell backwards over the bridge. Babs and Stew looked at each other and then screamed.

Stew, with his right foot bandaged and using one crutch, hopped out of the car and hobbled towards the railing as Babs ran around and joined him. They both looked out at the river in horror.

"Vivian!" Stew cried with both his hands flying through the air, expressing his distress. "Vivian!"

Babs was speechless as Stew continued to holler her name. He then burst into tears as Babs grabbed him for support.

"Vivian!"

There was a moment of silence.

Very faintly, they both heard from beneath them, "Stewie?"

Babs and Stew looked directly down. About two feet below the bridge was a workman's catwalk and Vivian was lying on it, flat on her back.

Without moving a muscle, Vivian smiled up at them. "Hey."

Stew wiped the tears from his eyes. "Can you move?"

"I don't think anything is broken."

Babs and Stew hung over the railing as Vivian reached up for their hands and they pulled her back onto the bridge.

Babs shook her head. "What the hell were you doing?"

"Resting?"

Stew blew his nose. "Damn. Next time can you rest about 100 feet closer to the ground?"

Babs was surprised at how little Vivian was wearing and how disheveled she looked. She gave her a tight hug and then pulled away.

"Gosh Viv," Babs exclaimed, "you're bone thin. When's the last time you ate something?"

"What year is it?"

Stew looked at her, very concerned. "That isn't funny."

Babs slipped her arm through hers. "We have to fatten you up." She looked to either side of the bridge. "Did you walk here? Where's your car?"

"I had to sell it," Vivian replied, flatly.

Stew pointed to the suitcase. "Is this yours?"

Vivian nodded as Babs walked her to the car and Stew picked up the suitcase. Surprised at how heavy it was, he grunted and almost dropped it as he stumbled with his crutch.

Babs turned around. "Stew, let me carry it." She took the suitcase from him as he limped back to the car.

Vivian pointed to his foot. "What happened?"

Babs shook her head and gave a look that implied don't go there.

Stew got back into the passenger's seat as Vivian slid into the back, squeezing in amongst a plethora of boxes.

Babs glanced at her watch, threw Vivian's suitcase into the trunk and hopped back into the driver's seat. "We're late for a party."

"I'm not in the mood to celebrate," Vivian said sarcastically.

Stew pointed to the boxes. "Tupperware. It's work."

"Are you still hawking that stuff?"

Babs turned around and gave Vivian a stern look. "If I take you home, will you promise to pick up the phone when I call and let me in when I visit?"

"No."

"What do you mean no?"

"I have no home. The bank took it."

Babs and Stew looked at each other. There was a momentary pause and then they both spoke in unison. "You're coming with us."

Babs started the engine, turned up the heat and drove across the bridge. Punchy from the whole ordeal and woozy from the warmth of the car, Vivian felt as though she were drunk.

Stew turned around and like a schoolboy, gazed at her. "Gee you're looking swell, Viv."

"No I'm not. I look awful. And what happened to you? Shoot yourself in the foot?"

Babs quickly looked over at Stew who spun back around and

glared out of his window. She then caught Vivian's eye in the rear view mirror and mouthed the words, "He shot himself in the foot!"

Embarrassed, Vivian dropped her head.

Babs drove off to Norwich as the three of them sat in silence and by the time they had pulled up in front of the hostess's house, Vivian had fallen asleep. She stirred as Babs and Stew proceeded to pull boxes out of the backseat.

"I'll just wait in the car."

"You'll freeze to death," Babs exclaimed.

"Who's throwing this party?"

Stew corrected her. "We're party dating with Olive Long."

Vivian was certain she was loosing her mind. "Who? What?"

Babs grabbed another box. "Her name is Olive Long."

"And we don't throw Tupperware parties," Stew added. "It's called dating."

"Well, that's right up Babs' alley." Vivian looked down at her soiled raincoat. "But I'm not dressed for a part...a date."

"There will be food," Stew winked at her.

Vivian perked up and started helping with the boxes.

~ ~ ~

In the living room of Olive Long's Tudor style house, sat 12 of her closest friends, all smartly dressed and laughing hysterically. Leading them through yet another game, Babs stood within the circle of women wearing a fitted wool jacket, a pencil skirt and pumps. The conservative look was a stretch for her, but she played the part sincerely and looked like she belonged.

Stew had set up a display of Tupperware items on the coffee table, which included stackable containers, pitchers, cups and bowls, all in an assortment of pastel colors. And at the far end of the room was a sideboard that displayed even more Tupperware. Some were full of hot casseroles, others of pretzels, peanuts, potato chips, miniature cakes and pies. There were also pitchers containing juices as well as hot coffee and tea.

And seated on a chair against the opposite far wall was Vivian. Having taken off her raincoat she looked completely out of place in her torn uniform. She had also, not so discreetly, removed her wet shoes and placed them on top of a sizzling steam radiator.

Babs spun around looking at each of the women who were holding their breaths. "And the winner is...Dorothy!"

She jumped to her feet screaming as Babs handed her a small bag. Dorothy excitedly pulled out a salt and pepper shaker, showing them off to everyone as they cheered and applauded.

Superficially, anyone looking in from the outside would have thought this was just a bunch of batty women getting all excited about some idiotic games where they could win kitchen gadgets. And yes, they were enjoying themselves. But something more important was happening here than just friends bonding together and having a party. What appeared to be insignificant plastic items were not only going to make their lives easier and more economical, selling these attractive products created the potential for each of these women, some, for the first time in their lives, to make their own money. Possibly a lot of money. And with money comes freedom, freedom on many different levels.

Right on cue, Stew balanced three large containers in one hand as he limped over to Babs. She winked at him acknowledging how great the party was going and placed them down onto the coffee table. The girls were all flirting with Stew and looking at him so sympathetically that Babs wondered if after his foot had healed, maybe he should keep up with the crutch and bum leg act.

Babs then looked at everyone very seriously as she placed her hands strategically on her hips. "Now if there's anyone here who doesn't have a kitchen, raise your hand now."

As all of the women laughed at the absurdity of the question, Vivian let out a quiet moan from the back of the room and raised her hand. Everyone turned around and stared at her.

Nervous, Babs quickly pulled them back into the next game.

"Ah...ladies...remember a Tupperware kitchen is well organized, efficient and neat. Let's play another game, shall we?" Babs gestured to the sideboard. "I hope this one doesn't ruin your appetites because we have delicious and fresh, hot and cold foods plus thirst quenching beverages just waiting for you to enjoy, after the games are over."

Vivian turned and looked at the stocked buffet.

Babs signaled all the girls to lean in closer to her as she whispered, "This one is called chubby bunnies."

The women chortled as Vivian quietly got up and walked over to the food. She eyed a stack of tiny finger sandwiches like she had never had a meal before in her life.

Babs opened up a sea foam green container of marshmallows. "This game is so much fun and we have another Tupperware prize to give away." She walked around the group of gals offering some to each. "Everybody, take one and when I say go, I want each of you to pop it into your mouth and let me hear you all say loud and clear, chubby bunny. Everybody ready? Go!"

Each of the ladies slipped a marshmallow into their mouths and all shouted out, "Chubby bunny!"

"Good girls!" Babs nodded to Stew who walked around with another container full of the spongy candy. "What we're going to do is keep adding them and whoever stuffs the most into their mouths and can still say chubby bunny, wins!"

The women screamed with delight as they stuffed another marshmallow in.

Babs hollered, "Go!"

"Chubby bunny."

Each of them stuffed another one in.

"Go!"

"Chubby bunny!"

Babs pointed to three women who couldn't enunciate it, and they were out of the game. The remaining players popped another one in.

"Go!"

"Chubby bunny," most of them slurred.

"No choking allowed," Babs warned them.

She pointed to four more to drop out and they played another round. "Go!" And Babs had to eliminate three more. "Only two of you left! Now gently, see if you can add one more marshmallow."

The women cheered the two on and once they had stuffed their cheeks like chipmunks, she pointed to the woman on her left. "Say chubby bunny."

She had to strain to make her tongue work. "Dwabba babba."

The women shrieked with laughter.

Babs pointed to her opponent on her right. "Say chubby bunny."

She took a dramatic pause and then said quite clearly, "Chubby bunny."

The room erupted into laughter as Babs touched her shoulder, crowning her the winner. Stew handed her a container to spit the marshmallows out into as Babs gave her a gift bag.

She pulled out the prize, looked at in awe and then waved it proudly up in the air as if it were an Olympic gold medal. "It's a butter dish!"

Babs led the girls in a round of applause. "And it's Tupperware that has kept these marshmallows delicious for…years!"

The women oohed and aahed.

Babs made a funny face as she picked up a container and its lid. "Seriously folks. Everything stays fresh because of the exclusive and patented Tupperware burping seal." She placed the lid onto the container. "Locks air, moisture and insects out, food flavors and values in! And watch." She lifted the corner of the lid allowing the air to escape with a whoosh. "Just burp it!"

Suddenly, a man-sized belch echoed throughout the room. All of the women plus Babs and Stew looked over at Vivian. She put her hand up to her mouth very ladylike and smiled. The entire stack of sandwiches was gone.

~ ~ ~

The date was a huge success and after Babs surprised Olive with a stylish Volupté compact courtesy of Tupperware for hosting the party, she, Stew and Vivian packed up all the demo pieces and headed back to her house.

As they reached the bottom of Mill Road and crossed over the wrought iron bridge, they took a sharp left just past the railroad tracks onto River Road. Along the north side of the street and facing the Drake River with no visual obstructions, was a row of classic Greek revival, mid-eighteenth century, mill worker houses with white clapboards and black shutters. And tucked right smack dab in the middle of these historic and exquisite homes was Babs', glaringly out of place, bungalow.

Built in 1910 and with its clapboards painted a dark brown and shutters a forest green, this pseudo craftsman style house with a giant wrap-around porch looked more suited for the lumber camps up north in the hinterlands than squatting on the edge of the Drake River in the bustling village of Abbot.

Tragically, Babs' and Stew's parents were killed in a car accident while Babs was a senior in high school, and upon graduation she started renting the two-bedroom house. Although it wasn't the prettiest ornament on the tree, it suited her needs especially since eight months earlier Stew appeared on her doorstep and wasn't showing any signs of leaving.

Once they had unloaded the Tupperware out of the car, Babs showed Vivian to the spare bedroom. "I was worried sick, Viv," Babs said as she pulled down the shade to the window. "Why didn't you pick up the phone? Why didn't you call me?"

Vivian lugged her suitcase into the room as Stew took the last of his clothes out of the dresser.

"Aw, Stewie," Vivian said, "I hate making you sleep in the living room."

"Not to worry, Viv. I'm glad to help." He limped out of the

room with his clothes.

Vivian turned to Babs. "I didn't call you because...I didn't want to feel like a charity case."

Babs was clearly tentative about how to deal with her. There was a moment of hesitation and then she put her arms around her. "You're not a charity case, you're my friend."

Vivian smiled and pulled away from her. Not wanting to mess up the bedspread with her dirty luggage, she opened it up on the floor.

Babs touched her dress. "Is this the uniform?"

Vivian smiled. "Still my favorite."

"Let me wash it for you."

Vivian looked down at the splattering of stains and the tear along her pocket. "I don't think it's worth it. I'd toss it but..." she pointed to the valise, "I'm not sure I packed another."

"Not to worry. I have plenty you can borrow. Let me get you some fresh towels and a robe."

Babs left the door ajar as Vivian unzipped her dress and let it drop to the floor. She stepped out of it, wearing a bra and half-slip. She unhooked the bra and took it off when Stew walked into the room.

"All stacked..." he said as he looked at Vivian's chest.

She screamed and covered herself with her arms. "Stewie!"

Totally embarrassed, he looked away and stood with his back to her, in the doorway. "The Tupperware is all stacked and put away."

Babs laughed as she came back down the hallway. "Back off, Casanova." He fled into the living room as she helped Vivian into a terrycloth robe. "Actually I think the two of you would make a cute couple."

"What?"

Babs shrugged her shoulders.

Vivian shook her head. "Oh I've always liked Stewie and his..." she brought her voice down, "...quirkiness. But the last thing I can think about right now is a man."

Both Babs and Vivian could hear him humming *The Man That Got Away* in the living room.

Vivian leaned into Babs and whispered. "Besides, haven't you wondered if he's maybe...he's a..." Vivian nodded her head.

Babs was totally at a loss. "A what?"

Vivian brought her voice down softer. "A homosexual?"

Babs repeated it at full volume. "A homosexual?"

Vivian shushed her as Babs started laughing.

"Darlin', how did you come up with that lamebrain idea?"

"He's sensitive, obsessed with show tunes and Judy Garland and he sells Tupperware."

"And that makes him a pansy?"

Vivian started gesturing in front of her face. "He uses his hands too much when he talks."

Babs really started to laugh as she spread a towel out onto the bed and put Vivian's suitcase on top of it. "You know he was married."

"And your point being?"

The two women chuckled.

Babs watched as Vivian started sorting through what belongings she had brought. "Stew's ex got the house so he's moved in with me till he gets his feet back on the ground. I have to admit, he's been here longer than I expected."

"Hotel Babs." Vivian paused for moment and looked at her very sincerely. "Thanks. You're a lifesaver. Literally."

Babs looked into the suitcase and saw that she had packed the framed picture of Paul that she kept on her night table. She searched Vivian's face for some reasoning and then decided not to push her. "You OK?"

"What do you mean?"

Babs held her hand. "The bridge and all."

"Just a momentary lapse in judgment. I'm fine now," Vivian declared rather weakly.

Babs pointed to the picture of Paul. "Have you seen him?"

A guttural sound of disapproval came up from her belly. "Today. But I haven't spoken to him since the divorce." She paused trying not to get emotional. "He asked for it and I wasn't going to contest so I offered to go to Reno for six weeks."

"A Reno-vation!" Babs exclaimed, trying to lighten up the mood.

"No. That wasn't fast enough for him. So he flew down to Mexico with…her…"

"Whatta slut!"

"And in 24 hours it was over and he and…"

"The home wrecker!"

"Were swimming and sunning and sipping piña coladas at some resort. Oh Babs, was I that horrible to live with?"

"No baby, of course not. He's the crumb."

"And I can't stop thinking about the fight Paul and I had before he left." Vivian started to cry. "The last thing he called me was…leftovers."

"What an ass." Babs put her arms around her. "Oh Viv, doesn't he realize that leftovers always taste better the next day?" That almost coaxed a chuckle out of Vivian. "Honey, how are you for money?"

"Twenty-five bucks to my name."

"Tonight I made almost $70."

Vivian turned to her. "Selling plastic?"

"Sometimes closer to $150 when I do two or three parties in a day."

"Babs, you could quit your receptionist job with that dentist."

"Nah, I love that gig. Just doing the parties for extra dough. Besides, I corral all my buyers in from the office."

This really got Vivian to thinking. "Geez, maybe I could…" she cut herself off with her own self-doubt. "No. You're so extroverted. A real people person. The thought of standing up in front of a group of strangers and talking mortifies me."

Stew knocked on the bedroom door and slid in with his back to the women.

Vivian laughed. "I'm decent."

Stew turned around singing, *"I'm always chasing rainbows, watching clouds drifting by..."*

He stopped abruptly, waiting for Babs to respond. Obviously this was a game Stew had tortured Babs to play, for years.

She thought hard. "Um, Mary Martin in *Peter Pan?*"

He threw her an exasperated look as his hands flew up with excitement. "I just bought at an estate sale the rare and almost impossible to find 12-inch 78 rpm recording of Judy singing the song *I'm Always Chasing Rainbows* from the 1941 movie *Ziegfeld Girl.* But that's not all. Included in the recording is the deleted reprise for the finale she did with Tony Martin. She's laughing and talking in between takes. Come into the living room and sing along!" Ecstatic, he left the room with his hands flailing by his sides.

Vivian gave Babs a look and they both broke out into laughter.

SIX

DUSTY BOOTS

The next day, Babs rushed through the living room looking for her purse as Stew limped in from outside on his crutch, teetering a box of Tupperware in his other hand. The sun reflecting in from the snow outside was blinding.

"It's a good thing this stuff is light," he laughed as he dropped it on the sofa. "Just picked up the new shipment. The garage is full."

Babs looked around the room at the Tupperware stacked and piled everywhere. "So is the house." She moved a few boxes around on the dining room table and finally found her handbag. "Let's hope business keeps up through the holidays."

Stew grappled with getting his overcoat off. "How is sleeping beauty?"

"Out to the world." She searched her purse for her keys.

"Babs, you didn't tell me Viv was divorced."

He hopped after her as she rushed into the kitchen.

"It just happened."

She looked left and then right and then opened the refrigerator.

"You should have told me right away."

She stared into the fridge. "What am I looking for? Keys!" She shut the door and shuffled things around on the wooden counter tops. "I'm sorry you weren't at the top of my divorce alert list." Frustrated, she jammed her hands into her pockets. She rolled her eyes, pulled out the keys and headed for the door. "Why don't you try cheering her up?"

He tagged after her. "How do I do that?"

Babs grabbed her coat and threw it on. "Just be your charming self."

"Ha ha."

"Show her your sense of humor. Gals always like that. I'm late." She opened the front door. "And get her out of bed before you hit on her, Mr. Lounge Lizard."

Babs winked at him and shut the door.

~ ~ ~

The shades were still drawn, blackening out Vivian's room. For the first time in weeks she had slept deeply and throughout the entire night. It was as if her body and spirit knew she was in a safe place. It also didn't hurt that the mattress, pillows and clean sheets felt like the most comfortable she'd ever slept in. Buried somewhere under the covers, she was out to the world.

Suddenly, she heard blaring music and two voices started to sing.

"Swanee, how I love ya, how I love ya, my dear old Swanee..."

In panic mode, Vivian bolted upright in bed, as if someone had blown off a shotgun.

"I'd give the world to be, among the folks in D-I-X-I-Even no' my Mammy's, waitin' for me, prayin' for me, down by the Swanee..."

Stew had slipped a recording of the sound track to *A Star Is Born* onto the 1945 Philco phonograph in the living room. Caught up in the song and joining in with Judy, he wasn't aware of how loud they were both belting.

"The folks up north will see me no more, when I get to that Swanee shore."

Wrapped in her blanket and with her hair wildly tangled, Vivian quietly appeared at the entrance to the living room and observed him.

"Swanee, Swanee, I'm coming back to Swanee. Mammy, Mammy, I love the old folks at home…"

Stew was just about to continue but Vivian cut him off by clapping. "Brava!"

Startled, he spun around looking at her. He threw up his hands and signaled that he would turn off the record player as Vivian shook her head.

"Was I that loud?" he shouted. He removed the needle and the house was quiet again.

"That could have wakened the dead."

"Aw, gee, I'm sorry," he said as he followed her into the kitchen.

If Stew's singing hadn't woken Vivian up, then maybe the red and white checkered linoleum floor would have. Or possibly the lime green painted kitchen cabinets. She staggered over to the built-in breakfast alcove and sat down as Stew rushed to her side.

Vivian shielded her eyes from the bright sunlight streaming in from the window. "Where are my sunglasses?"

"You hungry? I can whip something together. How about a fresh herb and vegetable frittata with sun-dried tomatoes or crème brûlée French toast with drunken strawberries or maybe just some simple eggs benedict?"

"Simple? How about a cup of coffee?"

Stew hopped to the kitchen counter and grabbed a mug. "There's some left over from earlier but I can make you a fresh pot if you prefer?"

"Stew, relax. That will be fine."

Stew took a deep breath, poured the cup of coffee and then carefully brought it back to the table and joined her.

Vivian took a sip as Stew watched her in silence. Feeling terribly self-conscious, she actually pulled her hair a little over her face as he continued to stare. She took it as long as she could and then blurted out, "Is there something wrong with me?"

Stew smiled from ear to ear. "You're just a…"

"Mess?"

"No!"

Vivian placed her elbows onto the table and dropped her head into her hands. "What am I going to do, Stewie? I'm destitute. I've searched this town high and low for a job but…"

"Do the Tupperware."

"I couldn't."

"Sure you can. I'd certainly be more than happy to help you in any way that I can."

"That's sweet of you but my life as I knew it has completely fallen apart and I just can't muster up the strength to do…anything."

Stew heard Babs' voice telling him to be his charming self and suddenly he had an idea.

"Well that's funny," he said as he reached out for her hand.

"My desperation is funny?"

"No." With his crutch in one hand and Vivian in the other, he clumsily guided her to the living room. "Um, I was just reminded of a very humorous incident that happened to me not too long ago. You want to hear it?"

"OK."

Stew pushed some of the Tupperware boxes off of the living room sofa and made room for them to sit. He turned and faced her with a warm smile on his face.

"A while back you may have heard that our grandpa Ross was diagnosed with cancer."

Vivian nodded very apprehensively.

"And after the doctors did all they could, they sent him home to die."

She nodded again but looked more frightened than apprehensive.

"Although Babs would disagree with me, I was his favorite grandchild and so I spent as much time with him as I could. So one day, we are just sitting in silence and suddenly he asks me, 'Stew, can you get a dying man a magazine?' And I said, 'Sure Gramps, what kind?' And he said, 'I want *Eyeful.*'"

This made Vivian's eyes open wide.

"'The one with Roma Paige on the cover,' he added. Now I loved my gramps so I granted him his wish, got the nudie magazine and rushed back to his room. He asked me to check where my grandmother was and I could see her outside pinning up the laundry. Then he told me to leave, closing the door behind me and come back in about 15 minutes."

Vivian's brow furrowed.

"So I did as I was told, watched the clock and maybe five minutes later my grandma comes back in and heads for the stairs. I tried to stop her but she wanted to check in on Gramps. She got to his room, put her hand on the doorknob, turned it, entered and…"

Stew just stopped talking. Vivian was about to fall off of the edge of the sofa. "And what?"

"Grandma screamed. On his lap was the opened magazine and a smile on his face. Gramps was dead."

Stew laughed so hard knowing he must have lightened Vivian's heavy heart with his keen sense of humor. For a split second her face was blank as she stared at him.

"It's true, Viv! Ask Babs."

Suddenly, Vivian's face scrunched up and she started to cry. Stew stopped laughing as she got to her feet and ran into her bedroom, hysterical.

Stew was completely confused. "Aw, geez."

~ ~ ~

The following week, with no other work options available and with an extra 10 bucks from Babs, Vivian broke down and purchased her Tupperware start-up kit for $35. In 1954, that was a lot of money considering the average American household made $3,960, a pair of nylons cost $1 and a gallon of gas was 21 cents.

A gigantic box was shipped to her from Florida and inside it was a suitcase full of Tupperware. Also included were very precise instructions on how to sell the products, sell yourself and maintain the bookkeeping. But the best thing she had going for her was that she had Stew and Babs to mentor her along the way.

Babs was driving her car down Main Street past the library with Stew squeezed in the back with the Tupperware while Vivian sat in the passenger's seat struggling with her demonstration speech.

"The Pie Taker provides easy transportation for all your desserts." She paused, hunting for the next word. She sensed Stew was about to tell her and like a traffic cop she halted his voice with her hand. "Don't tell me. It's something about popsicles. Um...everyone loves popsicles and now you can make your very own with Tupperware Ice Pops!"

Stew reached forward and touched her shoulder gently. "Ice Tups."

"Shoot! Why are they called ice tups?"

"Tups...Tupperware?"

Vivian was exasperated. "It still doesn't make sense to me."

Babs was just aching to talk. "So let me finish telling you about this guy I met, Kenneth."

Vivian checked her make-up in a compact mirror. "Babs, you always order the same thing: tall, dark and..."

"Disappointing," Stew added, laughing.

"Kenneth was married but she died. Very sad. He has two kids: Salvatore and Hannah."

Vivian chuckled. "Are they Italian or Jewish?"

Babs shrugged her shoulders. "Irish."

Stew and Vivian shot each other a glance.

Vivian turned back around and straightened out her simple green wool suit. She and Babs had searched her closet and although the button-down jacket and a-line skirt were almost a size too big, it was the one ensemble that fit the best. It came with a belt and would have looked more fitted if she had worn it, but Vivian held steadfast to her rule.

Feeling performance jitters, Vivian flailed her hands at Stew in the backseat. "What's after the popsicles?"

"Wonderlier Bowl sets," he shouted.

Babs couldn't help but cut in again. "Our next date he's taking me dancing."

Vivian looked at her with disbelief. "A second date?"

Stew leaned forward and stuck his head in between them. "This is a committed relationship."

Babs smiled. "But you'll never guess where he took me for my first date." She gestured to outside the window and slowed down the car as she approached the building.

Vivian sat up in her seat to get a better look. "What is it?"

Stew wiped the fog from his back window. "A restaurant?"

A slew of cars were parked in front of the establishment, underneath a giant golden arch. Across it was a red sign that screamed:

15¢

McDonald's

HAMBURGERS

We have sold OVER 1 MILLION

All three stared at the bizarre red and white striped building and the golden arches piercing through it.

Stew squinted. "McDonald's?"

"Kenneth says it just opened."

Vivian leaned forward to get a better look. "But why the golden arches?"

Babs stopped the car in front of the restaurant. "Maybe something to do with St. Louis? So he takes me inside and we're about to order and he says, 'I'm gonna buy a McDonald's.'"

Vivian clarified what she was saying. "A burger."

Babs shook her head. "No, the restaurant. They're going to try to sell ownerships across the country. And Kenneth also said he could get me some stock in the company on the cheap. Supposed to make a lot of money."

Stew rubbed at the steam fogging up his window again. "The sign does say we have sold over one million."

A car behind Babs honked its horn. She shifted the car and drove on, shaking her head. "I give this burger joint a year before it goes under."

Vivian grabbed a handful of tissue and stuffed it into Babs' oversized pumps she was wearing. "They're going to have to sell a lot more than just a million to make a good profit, yes? And what are the odds of that?"

Babs looked out towards the McDonald's one more time. "Maybe I'm a snob but I wouldn't be caught dead eating in a place like that, again."

They all laughed as Babs drove on.

~ ~ ~

Vivian had lost touch with almost all of her friends. She had rung up Gloria asking if she'd like to host a party and she said yes, but had to wait a week or two. So Babs very generously handed over her next party to Vivian.

As they pulled up to the hostess's house, Vivian's butterflies in her stomach flittered into extreme nausea. She jumped out of

Babs' car and restuffed the tissue into the shoes.

"Is it hot out here or is it me?" Vivian asked, fanning herself.

"It's you," Babs smiled as she popped the trunk and dragged out a box of Tupperware. Vivian took off her coat and threw it into the car as Stew carefully slid off the backseat to a standing position on the street. He had changed out the single crutch for a cane and wrapped his free arm around a box.

Vivian took out her compact again and her hand shook as she applied a layer of lipstick. She turned to them for reassurance. "You sure this looks OK?" she asked, straightening her skirt.

Stew looked at her, amazed. "You look so much better in that than Babs."

"Gee thanks," Babs said, elbowing him.

Vivian held her stomach. "I'm so nervous I think I'm going to throw up."

Babs handed her a box and then grabbed another one from the car. "Think of all of these women as your best friends. Keep it conversational and look them right in the eye."

Vivian repeated it in a whisper. "Right in the eye."

"And if you lose your place just take a deep breath and smile," Stew advised.

Vivian looked completely distressed as Stew winked at her. She crossed her fingers and sporting a half-smile she waddled up the walkway to the house, swimming in Babs' shoes.

Brother and sister gave each other a worried look.

~ ~ ~

In the living room, the ladies sat around Vivian as she held up six Tupperware Ice Tups in their tray. Looking even more distressed than before, Vivian started to shake as her mind went blank. She glanced to the back of the room for support from Babs and Stew.

Stew clearly mouthed the words, "Just take a deep breath and smile."

Vivian nodded, took a huge breath and then created a forced, wide grin of terror.

Babs reached for Stew's hand and whispered, "Oh God."

Vivian tried to talk through the smile as her upper lip quivered but instead of sounding friendly and reassuring, she unfortunately came off sounding scary and a bit mechanical. "Everyone loves popsicles and you can make your very own with..." she said the words slowly and deliberately, "...Tupperware...Ice...Pups."

The room broke into laughter. At first Vivian didn't know what they were responding to, then she heard what she had just said.

She laughed trying to make it seem like she meant to say it. "Oh, ah, Tupperware Ice Tups!"

Vivian put the tups down onto the coffee table and picked up a large and heavy Wonderlier Bowl full to the brim with macaroni salad. She held the container out in front of her and remembered what Babs had said. She then took her time and stared at each one of the ladies as hard as possible. Unfortunately, her attempt at a friendly connection came off like she was giving them the evil eye.

"Before we play the mimes Tupperware game I'd like to share with all of you the colorful and wonderful Wonderlier Bowl sets. They come in an assortment of pretty pastel colors, stackable graduating sizes and like all Tupperware products, the Wonderlier Bowls have a lifetime guarantee and keep foods airtight."

Amazed that she got through that entire part of the speech she nervously giggled but then fumbled trying to get the lid off of the Wonderlier Bowl. "Airtight. Very tight." She pulled with her right hand and then tried with her left. She took another deep breath. "Um...our food serving and storage containers are unbreakable and..." She stuck the bowl between her knees. "...Put economy in your kitchen and..." With both hands she pulled up with all her might. The lid flew off but so did the bowl from her knees, landing on the coffee table in front of the women, splattering macaroni salad all over them. "...Beauty on your table."

Vivian smiled hard and shook harder.

~ ~ ~

From the outside, Vivian, Babs and Stew could be seen sitting in the front window of the McDonald's eating burgers, fries and shakes, ravenously.

Babs counted out one-dollar bills onto the table in front of Vivian. "Here you go, honey. One, two, three, four, five, six, seven and eight."

Vivian looked at the money as she stuffed another fry into her mouth. "Gee, we're in the big time. Eight whole smackeroos. I'm surprised they bought that much."

Stew came up for air after noisily sucking his thick chocolate shake up through the straw. "At Babs' first party she lost money."

"It's true. I sold absolutely nothing and had to give the hostess 10 bucks for cost of food."

Stew pressed his forehead trying to relieve his instant cold drink headache. "Viv, next time you'll sell four times what you did today."

Having finished everything on her tray, Vivian licked her finger and started collecting every crumb she could find, to eat. "There isn't going to be a next time. The whole thing was so demeaning."

Babs sat up taller, closed her eyes and lowered her voice. "When you help someone up a hill you find yourself closer to the top."

Vivian stopped crumbing and stared at her. She looked at Stew and he smiled back. Thinking it was the show tune guessing game she thought for a moment and then asked, "Carousel?"

Stew laughed. "It's Brownie."

Vivian was at a loss. "A girl scout?"

He laughed harder. "No. The vice-president of Tupperware is Brownie Wise."

Vivian literally choked on her crumbs. "I don't know what's harder to swallow, that a woman is vice-president of a huge corporation or her name."

Babs stood up. "Well, I know what is easy to swallow, these burgers and fries. Another round?"

They all nodded.

~ ~ ~

Shell-shocked from her first party debacle, Vivian scoped out the rest of the shops and businesses in Abbot in hopes of finding a job. With no success, completely out of money and her debt to Babs and Stew growing every day, she broke down and reluctantly considered giving the Tupperware another chance. She had no choice.

That Saturday night Vivian sat on Babs' sofa surrounded by Tupperware with her head buried in a copy of Business Week magazine as Stew stood outside of the partially opened bathroom door talking to his sister.

"Babs," he whispered, "I'm going insane." He looked down the hall at Vivian. "I want to wrap my arms around her and tell her everything's going to be OK. Do you think I should?"

She whispered back. "Wrap your arms around her? No."

"Well then, what should I do?"

"Exude confidence."

Stew looked puzzled. "How do I do that?"

Babs opened the bathroom door enough to stick her head out, which was wrapped in a giant scarf. "You don't do it, you are it."

"I am?" he asked incredulously.

Babs shook her head. "What are we, in junior high? Stew, it's all about body language. Be spacious. A woman responds to a man who takes up as much space as possible."

"You do?"

"It's called being territorial. When sitting, lay back and relax.

Let your arms hang at your sides and make yourself as comfortable as possible. And when walking, no hands in your pockets and don't look down. Head up, chest out, shoulders back. And talk slowly." She looked at her wristwatch. "Now let me finish getting ready or I'll be late." She pulled her head back into the bathroom and slammed the door shut.

Stew stuffed his white button-down shirt into his beige chinos and then checked himself in the hall mirror. He licked both palms and tried to maneuver his bangs up and off his forehead but they had a mind of their own and were determined to lie flat on his forehead. He took a deep breath and then walked towards the living room.

Vivian turned a page in the magazine and held it up in front of her face. On the cover of Business Week was Brownie Wise. The caption below her picture read:

Brownie Wise of Tupperware, "If we build the people, they'll build the business."

No longer using his cane, Stew walked into the living room slowly and deliberately with his chest out, shoulders back and head up.

Vivian kept her face buried in the magazine, hearing him come in. "Did you know she's the first woman ever to be on the cover? There's a seven page spread here."

With his nose high in the sky, Stew bumped his shin into the coffee table. There was a second or two before he felt the pain. "Awww! Ohhh! Eeeh!"

"Watch yourself," she warned, still engrossed in the magazine and not looking up.

Stew cleared all of the boxes of Tupperware off the armless divan and sat down next to her. He spoke slowly. Very slowly.

"Re-mark-able. Here's the Tup-per-ware Sparks news-letter."

He handed it to her as he spread his legs as wide as possible and then dropped his arms to his sides as if they were paralyzed.

Vivian wondered why he was acting so strangely and then looked at the pamphlet. "Brownie looks like Betty Crocker. Is she a real person?"

Stew moved closer to Vivian spreading his legs even wider. "Oh, she's real all right." He inched a little bit closer to her and she responded by wiggling away. "Look," he said, nodding his head towards the newsletter instead of pointing with his finger. His arms continued to hang by his side, dead-like.

"Look at what?"

Stew nodded more aggressively with his head. "Open up the newsletter. It lists monthly top sellers and the prizes they've won."

She looked at his arms. "Did you hurt yourself, again?"

"Not at all."

He moved closer to Vivian forcing her to slide to the very edge of the sofa.

Her eyes got larger. "Wow, this woman got a new refrigerator!"

"Let me see."

He pushed even closer to Vivian compelling her to move away and suddenly she fell off the edge of the sofa and onto the floor.

Totally annoyed, she looked up at him. "What is wrong with you?"

Vivian stayed seated on the rug reading the newsletter as Stew let go of Babs' concept of territorial attractiveness. He could see the gears spinning in Vivian's mind. "What is it?"

"Brownie," Vivian said as she read on. "She says, 'Remember the steam kettle, though up to its neck in hot water, it continues to sing.'" That phrase resonated so strongly for Vivian. She put the newsletter down and looked up at him. "Stewie, I'm really going to work hard at this. I have no choice. And I'm going to succeed because I never, ever want to sink this low again in my life."

He smiled at her as he rubbed his foot.

"Viv, let's go over the spiel one more time."

"Your foot OK?"

"Just a little stiff."

She got back up onto the sofa and sat next to him. "Stewie, how did it happen?"

"You want the real story or the one I'm fabricating and will tell my grandchildren one day?"

She smiled warmly at him.

~ ~ ~

Almost six weeks earlier, Stew was walking his beat on a typical Saturday afternoon in Abbot. He thought it felt like one of those extraordinary days where there was a taste of each season in the air. The early morning dew had a fresh scent of spring in it while the noonday sun reminded him of the warm summer days that had just passed. But the late afternoon chill acknowledging the bountiful fall harvest also warned of the cold winter nights coming ahead. An avid reader with an eclectic taste in books, Stew remembered this type of day being described once in a tome about ancient Buddhist prayers.

Stew smiled. "It's a dojo day," he said quietly to himself as he walked a bit further on Park Street before turning onto Main.

Like honeybees sensing this was the last day to get work done before their long winter hibernation, the town was bustling with frenetic activity. With eyes and ears open, Stew oversaw everything, making sure the town and its people were safe and orderly.

A father and son entered Aquarius Hardware as a young mother and her daughter stopped to look at dresses displayed in McCartney's clothing shop. Suddenly, a group of teenage girls ran out of the Abbot Bookstore giggling, followed by just as many boys. But when Stew stopped for a moment and looked through the store window to see if any new books had arrived he heard a strange tapping sound coming from down the street.

He looked south on Main and saw an elderly blind man, some-one he had never seen in town before, walking towards him. Stew noticed that DeQuatro's restaurant, which was next to the book-store, had their metal sidewalk basement doors open, and the man was walking straight towards it.

Doing what any good cop would do, he rushed to the blind man's side.

"Excuse me, sir," he said very caringly.

But the old man tapped by him. "I don't need your help."

Stew stepped up to his side again. "I understand that but in front of you…"

He snapped at him. "Mind your own business!"

The blind man took a step closer to the open hole in the side-walk.

In the most authoritative voice Stew could project, he shouted to the man, "Sir, do not take another step."

But he did and that's when Stew grabbed the man's arm. The moment he touched him, the blind man went ballistic. He started waving his cane while swinging is left fist.

"Help!" he screamed. "Help, somebody help me! Is there a po-liceman around?"

A small crowd of people quickly gathered to see what the ruckus was about as Stew tried to protect the man without him-self, getting hit.

"Sir, I am a…"

"You are a stupid, stupid man. You are never to touch a blind person. Any idiot knows that, even a child. Let go of me!"

The blind man pulled his arm free from Stew and took a step closer to the grate.

Stew ordered him one more time. "Sir, stop or I'll have to…"

The man took another step forward and that's when Stew made the decision to stand in between him and the open pit down to the restaurant's basement. Upon bumping into Stew's chest, the blind man had a knee jerk reaction and pushed him out of the way. Stew tripped backwards over the open metal door and fell down into the basement. The moment he hit the ground, his gun went off.

~ ~ ~

Vivian had been hanging onto his every word. "My gosh, you're lucky you didn't break your neck!"

"Fortunately I landed on a giant bag of flour but I shot myself in the foot."

They looked at each other very seriously and then Stew burst into laughter followed by Vivian.

"Oh Stew, it doesn't pay to be nice."

"I'm lucky it only shot through soft flesh, just grazing my ankle bone." He paused for a moment, turning pensive.

Vivian studied his face. "Stew, why did you retire?"

He hesitated for a moment. "Retiring wasn't my idea."

"Were you forced?"

"Let's say, pressured. In hindsight, it's a blessing. Honestly, I'm not policeman material."

He said this with such complete acceptance and lack of self-pity that Vivian was totally moved and gently touched his hand.

Just then, Babs strutted down the hallway hollering, "Grab your partner!"

She entered the living room with her hair braided in pigtails and decked out in a red and white gingham pinafore dress, which had multiple layers of tulle puffing it out. With it she wore a shear white blouse with balloon sleeves and a Peter Pan collar. On her feet was a pair of chunky red velvet heels with giant polka dot bows.

She modeled the outfit across the room and back for them.

Vivian started laughing. "Where's the hoedown?"

"You're looking at her!" Babs squealed, pointing to herself.

Stew shook his head. "You look like a slutty Dorothy Gale."

Vivian laughed harder. "You're not going out of the house in that, are you?"

Babs gave them a twirl. "Yeah, I'm meeting Kenneth. He's playing fiddle for a barn dance up in Derry. Say, why don't the two of you come with? They're all so friendly and open to new dancers."

Vivian looked Babs up and down again. "I certainly don't have the wardrobe."

"We can whip up something together." Babs then turned to Stew.

"Don't look at me. I have two…no, one left foot."

"The doc said you have to exercise it."

Stew snickered. "But who the heck goes to a barn dance?"

Babs gave him a sarcastic look. "Um, I think a rather well known and beloved MGM star had a barn dance in certain movie called *Summer Stock*? I thought you were 'Mister Know It All' when it came to anything Garland?"

Stew knocked the side of his head for not remembering.

"And," Babs continued, "there'll be lots of free food."

Vivian stood up. "Did I hear free food?"

Babs gestured for both of them to come back to her bedroom. "It's recruitment night and I need to make my quota."

Vivian slipped her arm in hers. "OK Babs, now we understand the hard sell. First Tupperware, now barn dancing? What haven't you recruited?"

Stew laughed. "A husband."

Babs looked back at him. "Hey, I'm working on that too."

Stew pointed to her feet. "Are you gonna be able to dance in those Minnie Mouse shoes?"

"I hope not!"

~ ~ ~

The dancing trio piled into Babs' car and traveled north on Route

1 for about 45 minutes till they reached the town of Derry, New Hampshire. When they pulled up to the location, Vivian and Stew were surprised to discover that the dance was actually being held in a barn. A working barn.

Babs laughed. "Well, what the heck did you think a barn dance would be held in? A bread box?"

It was a mild and cloudless winter night with a full moon looking exceptionally large as it hung low in the sky just above the barn.

They all stepped out of the car and Babs took in a deep breath of the country fresh air. "Ah, what a night for a dance."

Stew looked up to the ominous looking moon. "Or a devilish murder."

Vivian shivered. "It does look a bit spooky."

"It's romantic," Babs said, correcting them.

The past two days had been so warm that most of the snow from the previous storm had melted so they took off their coats and left them in the car. Stew had thrown on a brown and yellow plaid shirt while Vivian was wearing Babs' white peasant blouse matched with a floral circle skirt with a petticoat underneath. Both had on their indestructible winter shoes.

Babs looked down at the muck on the ground and then at her red velvet shoes. "Why in God's name did I not wear my boots?"

Vivian shrugged her shoulders. "Slave to fashion?"

"You could jump on my back," Stew offered, "but I'm not sure I'm ready for that yet."

"What if Stew and I run in and find Kenneth?" Vivian suggested. "I bet he'll carry you."

"I don't think that's going to happen," Babs answered cryptically.

As lightly as she could step, Babs carefully tiptoed through the soft grass, hay and mud pies towards the barn.

The livestock were herded off to nearby pastures and machinery and tools were cleared out to make room for the dancing. And inside the centuries old barn were hundreds of twinkling Christmas lights intertwined with swags of pine bows strung from the rafters. And every window was framed with giant blue spruce wreaths decorated with apples and pinecones.

It was so beautiful that Babs, Stew and Vivian had to pause for a moment, taking it all in. As they entered the barn they noticed dozens of women setting out dishes of homemade food onto large tables flanking either side of the entrance.

Already in full swing were scores of people dancing in the middle of the barn. At the far end, performing on a platform, were the musicians playing a dulcimer, an accordion, a guitar, a bass violin and Kenneth with his fiddle. They were stomping out a classic New England barn dance song called *Road To Boston* as the caller in front of them hollered out the choreography to the dancers on the floor.

"Cuddle swing, switch," he shouted, "to a dead cat bounce!"

Hearing this, Vivian stopped in her tracks. "I think I'll allemande-left and do-si-do myself right out the door." She spun around and tried to leave when Babs and Stew slipped their arms through hers, spun her back around and dragged her into the dance.

Dressed in every conceivable barn dance outfit one could imagine, the dancers were spinning like tops.

"It looks like a kaleidoscope threw up," Stew said as he put his hand to his stomach.

Vivian shook her head. "Lord knows I can't do that."

"Relax," Babs reassured them, "this is an exhibition dance."

Along the outside perimeters, other newbies were seated upon bales of hay watching the seasoned dancers with great trepidation.

Vivian pointed to them. "Look at their faces. I bet they were ambushed like us, too."

The three of them worked their way down towards the musicians, passing by a woman dancing with great abandon. She was wearing a black jumper spotted with giant yellow and orange flowers separated by white lace, aqua ribbons and fuchsia panels.

Babs shouted out to her. "Loretta, love your outfit!"

"That dress is searching for a migraine," Vivian whispered to Stew.

He made a quick scan of everyone at the dance. "Viv, I think we're under the legal age."

"I heard that. Now stop it," Babs said as she gestured to the crowd. "Every barn dance organization has its own name."

"What's this," Vivian asked, "the Fallin' Arches?"

Babs smiled proudly. "The Dusty Boots."

Stew turned to Vivian. "Dusty they are."

The dance came to an end just as the three made their way down to the musicians. Everyone shouted and cheered as the white haired fiddler jumped off the platform, winced and instantly grabbed his knee.

"There's my guy!" Babs shouted as she waved enthusiastically to him.

Tall and handsome with a full head of snow-white hair, Kenneth was definitely looking a bit long in the tooth.

Vivian and Stew turned to each other. "Stew, I didn't know she was into older men."

"It was inevitable. She's dated everyone else in the North Shore."

Vivian laughed, hitting his arm as Babs pulled her beau over to them.

"Kenneth, this is my friend Viv and my brother Stew."

"Nice to meet you both."

Suddenly the caller shouted, "Everybody pair up, time for a contra dance. We're playing *Flowers Of Edinburgh!*"

"My fiddle's lead instrument in that one. Gotta get back to work," Kenneth said as he gave Babs a quick peck. He attempted to hop back onto the stage but lacked the strength. She ran over to him and pushed his butt back up as male dancers swarmed around Vivian.

A portly fellow grabbed her arm first and Vivian did a double take. He was a dead ringer for the actor who played Fred Mertz on the *I Love Lucy* television show.

Out of his pocket he pulled a nametag and a marker. "Name, doll?"

"Fred?" she asked, thinking it might actually be William Frawley.

"First time for everything." He wrote the name Fred down on the nametag and was just about to slap it onto Vivian's chest when she blocked his hand and grabbed the tag.

"I'll handle that."

She stuck the name Fred onto her blouse as he held out his hand for a shake. "I'm Rudy and you are now officially a Dusty Boot."

Vivian curtsied politely. "A dream come true."

The music started up again with the traditional Scottish tune.

Rudy placed Vivian into a row of women and then ran to the opposite line of men facing them. At the same time, a very large and masculine looking woman dragged Stew across the barn and plopped him next to Rudy as she zipped back to Vivian's side. And like a true groupie, Babs held back and stared up at Kenneth all dreamy eyed as he played his fiddle and stomped his foot. His good foot.

The caller tapped the microphone and then started. "Balance your partner and swing to your left, gypsy meltdown and swing to your right..." and instantly, all the new dancers veered off in all the wrong directions bumping into one another like human pinballs.

~ ~ ~

Having barely survived her first three dances, Vivian was having much more success at the refreshment table. With her newly declared commitment to selling Tupperware, her main concern was that she really had no friends to call upon. But to her amazement, she discovered that none of the women she was meeting at the dance had been to a party. In fact, none of them were even familiar with the products. Vivian wrote her name and Babs' phone number down on a piece of paper and handed it to the woman dishing out helpings of her holiday spaghetti casserole.

"Debbie, Tupperware will keep all this food fresher, longer."

"And if I host a party, you said I get free Tupperware?"

"Yes. In fact, you can become a Tupperware lady yourself if you like. Maybe you want some extra money for that new hat or a pair of shoes? Or the kids might need something important?"

Debbie handed the plate of spaghetti to Vivian. "So you make good money doing it?"

"You get out of it what you put in." Then Vivian paused, wanting to quote Brownie perfectly. She continued a bit stiffly. "A still pool…of water stagnates more…rapidly than a running stream."

Debbie was a little confused. "OK."

Then Vivian snapped back to her warm self. "Just give me a call and we'll set something up."

"Gee, thanks. I will."

Vivian took her plate of food over to a bale of hay and watched as a sprightly octogenarian out on the floor swung Babs around a little too aggressively. They switched partners and another man reached out for Babs but clearly got two handfuls of breasts instead of her waist.

"Ahhh!" Babs shrieked. She stopped dancing and squinted at his nametag. "Mister Dimitri Romano, watch it with your Russian hands and Roman fingers!"

She bowed out of the dance and dizzily stumbled over to Vivian who was laughing. "Babs, I didn't know barn dancing was a contact sport."

Babs plopped herself down on the hay. "I think I made his night."

"His year."

"Isn't it fun, Viv?"

"It's different."

"So what do you think of Kenneth?"

"I think you're smitten."

"You don't like him."

"I don't know him. He's certainly a bit older than the guys you usually date."

"Is that a bad thing?"

"No, considering they all turned out to be losers. But like you say, the important thing is that you're happy."

"Hmm. Am I?"

Vivian nudged her as they looked out onto the floor and watched Stew struggling through a dance. Trying to spin in a Dixie wheel formation, he got flustered and screwed everything up so that his group had to stop dancing. Vivian and Babs started giggling as Babs slipped off her shoes and rubbed her feet.

"Oh Viv, it's so good to see you out, laughing and enjoying yourself."

"This really is a hoot."

"And who knows, maybe you'll relax, take off your spurs and end up dancing with the man of your dreams."

"Nah, this cowgirl is out of the saddle."

The caller hollered out, "Rip cord!" and Stew was flung into a sea of spinning women.

~ ~ ~

After several more dances and seconds on the food, Babs and Stew were ready to call it a night but Vivian was still working the room.

"Thanks Carol. I'll call and we'll set something up."

Babs and Stew waved to her as she handed her name and number to another woman. "Here you go, Paula."

Vivian caught up with them at the front door and then turned back and waved to another. "Love your dress, Betty!"

From the back of the barn, Kenneth signaled Babs to come over. "Let me say goodnight to him one more time."

She ran back to him as Rudy came up to Vivian.

"Do I get your number too, Fred?"

"Sorry," she said, smiling. "This is work."

Stew slipped his arm through Vivian's as she looked back to the other women. "Bye everyone!" She leaned her head into Stew's. "Thanks for rescuing me. How's your foot?"

"Actually feels good."

"Now where were we?"

"The Tupperware Handolier Cannisters are..."

"One of a kind!"

Stew beamed from ear to ear as they walked out together into the moonlit night.

SEVEN

SHOWTIME!

"I'm shaking like a bowl of Jell-O," Vivian confessed as she paced Debbie's kitchen. With Babs working at the dentist's office Stew helped Vivian set up for the Tupperware party.

"Viv, you're going to be fine. We've rehearsed this inside and out."

The women waiting for her in the living room burst into laughter, which made Vivian tremble even harder.

Debbie stuck her head into the kitchen. "Ready Viv?"

She adjusted the same green suit she had borrowed from Babs for her first party and then cleared her throat. "As much as I'll ever be."

Stew bowed and gestured to the door. "It's showtime!"

In the center of the living room was a card table covered with a white tablecloth overflowing with Tupperware products. There were more items stacked on the coffee table, end tables and on top of the buffet along the back wall of the room. Six women were squeezed onto the sofa while another fifteen sat in easy chairs, folding chairs and even on pillows thrown onto the floor.

Debbie walked in and to the center of the room. "Girls, it's time to have some fun." They all applauded and cheered. "My new friend Vivian has been so kind to come to my home today to share with all of us the wonderful world of Tupperware." The gals cheered even louder. "So here she is, Vivian Lawson."

Just about to enter, Vivian spun around and embraced Stew with a huge hug. She picked up a tray of Tupperware, said a prayer and then entered the living room. Not surprisingly, her spontaneous and unexpected display of affection hurled Stew into heaven.

At the beginning of the demonstration, Vivian veered from the suggested way to run the party and decided to pass out a dessert plate to each woman and offered them a choice of cake, pie, tarts or chocolate to make them feel special and welcomed. And it worked. It broke the ice and the women loved it, however it temporarily distracted them from what she was saying.

But once she had their full attention again, something wonderful started to happen. Vivian discovered a quality she never really knew she possessed. She had a self-deprecating sense of humor and it wasn't an act she was putting on, she was just being herself. And to her delight, the women were responding to it in a very positive way.

"Girls, the truth is, I'm terrible in the kitchen."

The women laughed at this which momentarily threw her off because she was dead serious.

"I mean it. My husband left me because my cooking was so bad."

This made them laugh even harder. Vivian trusted her instincts and just went with it.

"Can you imagine if I had Tupperware back then? All those awful meals I threw together, and I mean literally threw them together, would all still be fresh!"

The gals couldn't keep it together, they found this so amusing.

"But I also keep dry goods in my Tupperware." Vivian picked

up a pitcher. "In these handy Handolier Pour and Store Pitchers with waterproof flip-top spouts, I fill them with cereal, dried pasta, even nuts. I also keep my laundry detergent in them."

She picked up a round container.

"And these stackables are also great for storing sewing supplies. And don't forget the men in your lives. Store their hooks and flies for fishing in these or nails, nuts and bolts. Say, do you all want to play another game?"

"Yes!" they all hollered.

"OK, this one is called Musical Tupperware but before we start I want each of you to carefully look underneath your dessert plate, carefully if there's still a delicious taste treat on them, and tell me if you see anything."

The ladies held up the plates and looked at their bottoms.

A woman sitting in one of the easy chairs jumped to her feet. "Mine says winner!"

The group cheered as Vivian handed her a small bag. "Then this must be yours."

Beyond excited, she reached for the bag, pulled out a tissue wrapped item and tore it open. Describing it like it was worth a million dollars she declared, "Look! I won…a funnel! Can you believe it? A funnel!"

The girls all laughed hysterically as Vivian smiled with confidence.

~ ~ ~

After all the women had left, Stew boxed up the Tupperware as Vivian counted out the money on Debbie's coffee table.

"One hundred ninety-six, ninety-seven, ninety-eight!"

Debbie was amazed. "Oh my Lord!"

"And Debbie," Vivian added, "you get to keep the Dip and Serve Serving Tray, the Wonderlier Bowls, the Handolier Canisters and the Bye Fly Flyswatter."

Surprised, her hands flew to cheeks. "Just for hosting?"

Vivian reached out for her hand with genuine affection. "It's a *thank you* for hosting."

"Oh Vivian, I have lots more friends to tell about this."

"Just let me know when you want to have your next party."

She walked Vivian and Stew to the front door. "Thank you. Thank you both so much."

Vivian turned back to her. "Stew, myself and Tupperware thank you. Bye Debbie."

Debbie closed the door as Vivian and Stew walked towards his car. Suddenly Vivian let loose and started dancing with him on the front lawn.

"I did it!"

"Vivian, you were amazing."

"I did it, Stewie! I really did it!"

She kissed him on the cheek and then twirled around Debbie's front lawn laughing. Stew couldn't have been happier.

~ ~ ~

The success of the party was exactly what Vivian needed to propel her forward and tap into a self-confidence she had never really felt before. She quickly threw parties with all the women she had met at the barn dance but then things came to a halt. She had to discover new people to "date". Better yet, if they became dealers they could earn their own money while Vivian received a commission.

It was while reading an issue of the Tupperware Sparks newsletter sent out by Brownie, that Vivian solved her problem. In it Brownie addressed Vivian's exact problem and the solution was "Operation Doorbell". The concept, which initially was frightening and daunting to Vivian, was cold pitching. She had to go door-to-door touting the plastic products with the concept of sharing it with friends. In the beginning, no doors were slammed in her face but many would quickly say no, thinking she was a Fuller Brush woman, wanting money for the heart drive or selling all occasion greeting cards. But Vivian persevered and honed her speech and quickly her little black book was filling up with dates all through the month of December. Not just one party a day, but sometimes up to three and four. And by her side and very eager to help her along the way was Stew, setting up and breaking down the demos as they ran from house to house.

It was 10:20 A.M. on a Thursday morning and Vivian was already halfway through her first party of the day at Carla's house located on Sunset Rock Road. She stood before a gathering of 15 women.

"The only thing worse than my cooking is my sewing!" she declared as she held up a darned sock full of holes.

The women giggled as she stuffed it into her pocket and held up a very small Tupperware bowl with a lid.

"Wonderlier Midgets! Have you ever seen anything cuter?"

The women applauded as Vivian easily opened it up and passed it around.

Vivian and Stew just barely made it to their next date, which was held at 3:00 P.M. at Ronnie's home on Hidden Road. The living room was full of 18 women laughing uncontrollably.

"The only thing worse than my sewing is my ironing!" Vivian said, deadpan, which made them howl even louder.

She then held up two drinking cups. "Tupperware Bell Tumblers. Your kids will love them!"

The women started to applaud.

At 6:35 P.M. she was demonstrating in front of 12 women and 2 men at Gertrude's house on Central Street.

"The only thing worse than my ironing are my organizational skills," she proclaimed, making a sour looking face.

The room laughed as she held up a tightly sealed bowl full of water.

"That's where Tupperware makes my life so much easier. All

items seal tight, are colorful, flexible, compact, child safe and…"
She threw the bowl full of water to one of the men and he caught
it. "Spill proof!"

At 8:00 P.M. Vivian and Stew held their last party of the day
at June's house situated on Randall Avenue. An astonishing number of 22 people showed up. She stood before them holding a
Wonderlier Bowl full of fresh fruit.

"I may be organizationally challenged but I never come up
short with my maternal instincts."

Vivian caressed the bowl, gently tapped its side and then easily
lifted the lid and burped it.

Everyone broke out into laughter.

"There, there," she said as if it were a baby. "They are lightweight, indestructible and never sweat." Vivian wiped her forehead with her arm. "Unlike me."

Everyone laughed as Vivian winked at Stew in the back of the
room.

~ ~ ~

Finally, Vivian had a day off and to celebrate she slept.

Stew had dragged a Christmas tree into the house earlier in
the day and set it up in the living room. He and Babs had already
strung the lights upon it but were holding off on the ornaments.

Early that evening, Vivian was still out to the world when
Babs knocked on her door.

Vivian sat upright blurting out, "Wonderlier Bowls…inde-
structible!"

Babs lost it laughing and laid down next to her on the bed.
"You're selling Tupperware in your sleep?"

Vivian was completely disoriented. "My life went from pathetic to plastic."

"You betcha!" Babs exclaimed. "You're a selling sensation."

Vivian laid back down next to her. "I feel like I haven't seen you in weeks."

"You haven't."

"How are you? How's Kenneth?"

"As you know, he was sweet and all but he finally told me his real age."

"And?"

"Viv, I was dating a man older than my father."

"Is that legal?"

Babs chuckled. "And his kids have kids."

"Granny Babs."

"So I met this guy last night. Very handsome, attentive banker but…"

"But what?"

"But he asked me how I felt about him shaving."

Vivian sat up in bed and asked tentatively, "His face?"

"No," Babs said wondering if she should go on. "Down there."

"Down there, where?"

Babs paused for a dramatic affect. "Way down there. He says it's all smooth as a baby's bottom."

"Ewwww!"

Stew knocked on the door and stuck his head in, looked at Vivian and started humming *Have Yourself A Merry Little Christmas*.

She looked to Babs for help who indicated she was on her own with this one. Stew continued to hum as Vivian wracked her brain thinking of all the Garland movies she had seen.

"Um…*The Pirate*?"

He shook his head.

"Oh wait! *Girl Crazy*?"

He continued to hum.

"I've got it. *The Harvey Girls*?"

"You're hopeless," Stew said.

Babs came to the rescue. "*Meet Me In St. Louis*."

"There you go," Stew laughed. "But what's the song?"

Vivian dropped her head. "I'm not a big movie fan like you are."

"Viv, everyone knows this one," Babs said, tickling her side.

Stew added, "Especially considering the date."

Vivian was at a loss. "What's today?"

Babs and Stew looked at each other and in unison said, "Christmas Eve?"

Vivian bolted out of bed. "You're kidding me?"

They both shook their heads.

"But where did the time fly?"

Babs led her out of the bedroom. "You've been working your tail off."

Stew followed them into the living room.

"Oh my gosh," Vivian said, astonished. "You put up a tree!"

Babs pointed to a box of ornaments. "We thought you'd like to join us in decorating it. Let me just run up to the attic and get the other box."

Vivian followed Stew into the kitchen. "Viv, let me cook you up something. You must be starving."

"Don't go out of your way."

"This is my creative outlet. You just woke up so how about some blueberry and Grand Marnier buttermilk pancakes?"

He went to the fridge as she sat down at the alcove table.

"Stew, how did you learn to cook like this?"

"Out of necessity."

She laughed. "I had necessity but that didn't help." He smiled as she watched him grab some eggs, milk and butter. "Stew, why did she leave you?"

He paused and looked out of the kitchen window. He was going to change the subject and tell her that gigantic snowflakes were now falling outside but instead, decided to answer her.

"Because she fell out of love with me." He turned around, looking at her. "Honestly, I don't think she ever loved me. I was her escape from a very domineering mother."

Vivian laughed to herself, knowing all too well.

He grabbed the canister of flour. "But she'll say she left because she couldn't take the pressure of being a cop's wife."

"I can understand that."

"Well, it's ironic that she divorces me and then I lose my job."

Vivian watched him as he started mixing the pancake ingredients. "Stew, did Paul have anything to do with that?"

"Not directly but he certainly campaigned as hard as he could."

"What do you mean?"

"Paul has an outrageous sense of entitlement. Especially when…" he hesitated, questioning whether he should say anymore.

"It's OK. Go on."

"Especially when it comes to women. He abused his power, both as a man and a police officer, to seduce them. I think some of them were frightened not to have sex with him, which is horrific, and I told him so. I'm sure he was worried that I'd go to the top and snitch on him but I would never have done that. Still, he made sure that I was out of the picture. Sorry Viv, the man's a pig."

"Trust me, I found that out the hard way."

Babs reappeared with the box of ornaments and put it on the table. "I think this is all of them."

Stew went over to the box. "There are a few here that are my favorites." He gently took a tissue wrapped ornament out and opened it up, showing it to Vivian.

She touched it carefully. "A miniature crate of oranges."

Stew dug through the box. "There's a bushel of plums and another one of lemons. Not sure why I love them so much."

"I think maybe cause you adore food?"

"Viv," Babs said, "in honor of your presence on this Christmas Eve night, I think you should be the first to hang an ornament."

Just then, Vivian's tears started to flow. Babs and Stew looked at each other, worried.

"It's OK," she reassured them. "They're tears of joy. It's just that…I've never done this before."

Babs hugged her. "Well, we should have invited you over before."

"No, I mean, I've never decorated a tree before."

Babs and Stew looked at each other again.

Vivian smiled. "This isn't a sob story. It's just the truth. When I was a child, every year the fake tree went up fully decorated. Then when my father died, trees and gift giving disappeared altogether except for in the servant's quarters. The maids always put up a scrawny tree but I was never allowed to go near it."

Babs shook her head. "There oughta be a law."

"And Paul's an atheist…"

"Figures," Stew said, with contempt.

"So we never celebrated."

Stew picked up the box of ornaments and they followed him to the tree. "Well, tonight will be your virgin tree trimming." He handed her the miniature crate of oranges.

"But this one is your favorite, you should…"

"No," he said cutting her off as he went over to the phonograph. "You should."

Vivian looked at the two of them a bit helplessly. "Do I just put it anywhere?"

Babs smiled warmly as Vivian hung it front and center and Stew slipped on an LP of Judy singing *Have Yourself A Merry Little Christmas*.

EIGHT

JUBILEE

Vivian learned the hard way that no one wanted to sell, buy or host Tupperware between Christmas and New Years. But she had already become addicted. Addicted to the adrenaline rush she felt when a party was a success. She loved the laughter generated at the get-togethers but more importantly she felt a great sense of satisfaction knowing she was helping to change their lives for the good. Plus, the "dates" had become her social life.

Not wanting to lose the steam she had built up, she spent her downtime studying her Tupperware manuals and Brownie's mantras. Once the holidays were over, she resumed her "Operation Doorbell" but also started phoning up past party hosts to see if they'd like to book additional parties. Vivian also got quite creative with her marketing schemes.

One day she filled the backseat of Stew's car up with Tupperware, but not in their boxes, she just towered everything up to the roof of the car. She had Stew pull into a gas station and just as she suspected, the gas station attendant asked what was in the backseat. This was all Vivian needed to gently slide into her soft-sell pitch and when the man realized how much money she was making, he exchanged phone numbers with her wanting to share this concept with his wife.

Vivian used this technique time and time again with terrific results. It really worked successfully in supermarket and department store parking lots as husbands patiently waited for their wives to finish errands. Vivian would have Stew park next to their cars and Vivian would open the backseat door and start stacking Tupperware into her arms until she was just about to drop them. Eventually the men would notice, jump out of their cars to assist and then Vivian would go into the pitch again.

At first, Vivian felt a twinge of deceit but the end result would be a win/win for everyone. Not only were the men eager for their wives to make extra income but some even moonlighted on the side or quit their jobs altogether to help with the distribution of items, like Stew did.

Soon Vivian was selling full force again but even stronger. She created what she called the "six-party-fete". Starting at 9:00 A.M. she held parties at two-hour intervals with the last one beginning at 8:00 P.M. With two sets of displays, Stew would help Vivian set up the first party. Then he would drive to the next location and set up for the next date while she was demonstrating. He'd rush back to Vivian and when the first party had finished, he'd pack up the display, drive her to the second party while he drove on to the third. They would hopscotch like this until they had finished the last party of the day. Then they'd drop by McDonald's at the end of the evening for burgers and fries and tally up the orders and money they had made. Vivian found this hectic schedule simultaneously exhausting and exhilarating. For the first time ever, she had control of her life. She felt self-confident and independent.

Vivian kept up this insane pace for the next three months and in early April she was thrilled to discover that she had been invited to her first regional gathering of Tupperware dealers to be held at the historic Bulfinch hotel in downtown Boston.

Vivian had read about the meetings in the Sparks newsletter. The year before Babs and Stew had attended for their first time. They were like pep rallies where dealers and managers from the surrounding areas could socialize, strategize, win prizes and have a hell of a time partying.

With her hard earned money, Vivian broke down and bought herself some new dresses. Babs tagged along as her personal stylist, which may or may not have been a good idea. It was obvious that Vivian was pretty conservative and hadn't a clue about fashion but on the other hand, Babs was far out there with her style choices and always eager to shock. But together they managed to find a few items that felt comfortable to Vivian. Nothing was cutting edge but pieces that seemed appropriate for selling Tupperware.

Although she questioned how fashionable one of her buys would be for the convention, considering her unforgettable induction into the Dusty Boots barn dancing club, Vivian chose to wear her new petticoat dress. Supposedly all the rage in the spring of 1955, she actually loved how it flattered her figure. Having gained a few pounds in the last couple of months, she had some curves to her body not too mention, bosoms.

The short-sleeved blue floral print acetate dress with rhinestone button trim at the neckline had an umbrella skirt with stitched tucks all around that gave her the new smooth hipline that all the gals wanted. And the separate taffeta petticoat had a blue hue that just teased out under the skirt. With matching faux jade earrings and necklace, she finished off the look wearing white kid gloves and a pair of teal blue pumps with a kitten heel. Although the entire ensemble cost her $37.98, which included a new handbag, she felt like a million bucks.

Babs drove down to Boston in her car as she and Stew tried to answer the hundred and one questions Vivian was asking about the regional meeting and what was going to transpire. The

Bulfinch was located in the north end of town on Merrimac Street but while talking up a storm, Babs missed a turn and they unexpectedly ended up on none other than Pinckney Street.

Vivian's nonstop chatter came to a complete halt when she saw a much-aged Maid 4 sweeping the front stoop of her mother's townhouse as they drove down the cobblestone street. She wanted to stop and say hello but sensing her mother might be at home she decided against it, not wanting to put a damper on the celebration.

And when asked why she had become so quiet she just laughed it off and said, "The anticipation of the event is so...overwhelming."

But seeing Maid 4 filled Vivian with an odd combination of emotions. She felt a deep feeling of loss and sadness mixed with a profound sense of freedom and new beginning. Just as they were passing by, Maid 4 looked up and Vivian quickly spun around, wondering if she had recognized her.

After backtracking up to Merrimac Street and finding a parking space, the trio rushed into the historic flatiron building that was already teeming with dealers from all over New England. Once they were checked in, they all headed to the enormous conference room. Round tables were beautifully set for dinner and down in front was a makeshift stage with folding screens on either side. Above it hung a large banner:

WELCOME

New England Regional Dealers and Managers

Tupperware

April 1955

Babs, Vivian and Stew were lucky to find three seats together but mid-way through the ceremonies, Stew seemed to disappear.

Esther Gaffney, the hostess of the evening, reappeared and walked up to a microphone set up center stage.

"Thanks to Barbara Manning for those clever tips to help you all sell your Tupperware," she said as she looked off towards one of the partitions.

The audience applauded as Vivian turned to Babs. "Where did Stewie go?"

"You'll see him in a moment," she said with a mischievous smile.

Esther motioned to the audience to quiet down. "Before we announce this month's top sellers we have a special announcement from three of our most beautiful Tupperware ladies ever to grace this stage." She looked off to see if they were ready. "Let's give a big round of applause for none other than...Polly, Bobbie and Stewina!"

Two men, Paul and Bob, wobbled out onto the stage dressed in drag. Both of them were wearing matronly floral housedresses, wigs and painfully high heels. As the audience erupted into laughter, it was obvious that someone was trying to push Stew onto the stage. He ran off and then was pushed back on and suddenly his attitude changed. He strutted, in the sexiest way that he could, towards the other two men. The audience lost it when they saw him wearing a black Frederick's of Hollywood off the shoulder cocktail dress and matching opera gloves. He teetered in black high heels, wore a black wig and had stuffed giant balloons into his chest.

Vivian's hands went up to her mouth. "Oh my Lord!"

Babs turned to her. "I don't know when it started but it's a running gag with every regional meeting across the country. And it was the guys' idea!"

Babs and Vivian looked at each other and broke out into laughter.

Paul stepped forward and held up a pink round plastic box and in a falsetto voice said, "Mr. Tupper..." The audience flipped over his voice. When they calmed down enough, he continued. "Mr. Tupper has created an assortment of new products like this boiled egg keeper." He opened the lid. "The perfect solution for getting those devilish…" Bob slaps Paul on the behind and almost drops his Tupperware full of eggs. Again, the audience roared. "The perfect solution for getting those devilish eggs to the picnic in good condition."

Paul stepped back as Bob took a step forward holding a large orange plastic key. In an even higher voice he squeaked, "And how about…" the audience cut him off with laughter. "And how about this beautiful Tupperware wall key chain holder? A place to store the key…to my heart."

He held it up against his heart as Stew and Paul gave him a sandwich hug, rubbing their breasts all over him. Bob stepped back and Stew wobbled forward. He waited for them to calm down and then said in the deepest bass voice he could conjure up, "Or how about…" the audience laughed as Babs and Vivian doubled over. "Or how about this fashionable combination?" He held up a large comb and started stroking his wig. "A comb to keep your locks shining and tangle free?" He struggled as the comb got caught in his hair and had to yank it out, almost pulling off the wig. He flipped the comb around and looked into its mirror. "And look! A mirror to admire your handsome, ah, pretty face in." He mugged into the mirror and started singing *I Feel Pretty* from *West Side Story*.

The audience went wild as Stew then stopped singing and stared into his reflection. "Mirror, mirror on the comb, who's the fairest Tupperware lady in my home?"

The audience cheered him as he and his cohorts curtsied and ran bow-legged off stage.

Esther reemerged pointing towards the men. "Let's hear it for Paul, Bob and Stew." Everyone clapped as she continued. "So make sure you check out the display in the back of the conference room and put in your orders as soon as you can."

Vivian leaned in to Babs. "Gotta run to the little girl's room."

Vivian stood up and squeezed by people and chairs as Esther continued.

"And now I have the pleasure of announcing this month's top sellers. I want our runner-up to claim her very own General Electric portable 100 watt 3 speed electric mixer...and it's Sally Connor!"

The room cheered as Sally jumped out of her seat, which was at the back of the room, and practically mowed down everyone in her way as she tried to make her way to the stage. "Thank you!" she screamed. "Thank you ever so much!"

Vivian reached the back doors but stopped when she heard the audience laughing. She turned around and saw an exuberant Sally trying to hop up onto the four-foot high platform but it was just too tall for her. Like a Jack Russell terrier she kept leaping into the air until an attendant ushered her over to the side and helped her up the stairs. Beyond excited, she tripped running up onto the stage.

Esther handed the mixer to Sally who almost dropped it and then she was escorted off the platform. Vivian pushed through the exit doors as Esther continued.

"And our top seller for this quarter is..."

Vivian searched the hotel lobby for the ladies room as she heard cheering and applause coming from the conference room. She was just about to ask the concierge where the bathroom was when Babs came flying out.

"Vivian! Vivian!"

She turned around.

"It's you!"

"It's me, what?"

"You won! You have to go up on stage!"

"I won what?"

"Top seller!"

"Aw geez, but I really have to go to the..."

Babs dragged her back into the conference room. When Vivian entered, the entire audience stood up and applauded, as Babs pulled her towards the stage.

Esther gestured out to Vivian who was winding her way around the tables down to the front of the room. "Ladies and gentlemen, one of our newest members and definitely our newest top seller, Vivian Lawson!"

Unlike Sally, the moment for Vivian was so surreal it was as if she were walking in slow motion. Babs guided her over to the stairs and pushed her from behind.

"Viv, get your butt up there!"

As Vivian walked across the stage she could see Stew off to the side still in his drag outfit, attempting to jump up and down in his high heels, giving her the thumbs up.

Esther embraced Vivian and brought her over to the microphone. "Before we present you with your reward, I have a little something here that might excite you."

The audience oohed and awed as she handed Vivian a letter and encouraged her to open it. It seemed like an eternity passed before she managed to open the envelope and then a silence fell over the audience as she quickly scanned the note.

Vivian looked as though she were about to faint.

Esther laughed, putting her arm around her for support, and then addressed the audience. "When Vivian stops pinching herself, she'll tell you what it is."

Esther encouraged her to read it but Vivian shook her head, indicating she was completely speechless. Everyone held their breath as she regained her composure and then read the letter.

"Dear Vivian, congratulations on a job well done. I personally track everyone's performance on a weekly basis and I must say you are one talented and busy young lady. Here's a gift from Tupperware to say thank you for all your hard work. I'd also like to extend my personal invitation to you to join me in celebrating Tupperware's next Jubilee down here in sunny Florida." The audience cheered as Vivian continued. "What lies behind us and what lies before us are tiny matters compared to what lies within us. Job well done. Best Wishes, Brownie Wise."

Just then, a giant portrait of Brownie unrolled down from the ceiling. Everyone started cheering and applauding.

Esther tried to speak over the roar. "And your prize is…" The curtains behind them opened up and the crowd went insane. "A brand new Maytag automatic washing machine!"

Vivian was stunned. She barely had the strength to walk over to the prize and when she did, she touched it gently, as if it were the most precious thing she had ever seen. The audience laughed as Babs cheered from the bottom of the stairs and Stew watched proudly from the wings.

Esther brought the microphone over to her. "I'm so excited," Vivian said, trembling. "I think I'm going to have an accident."

Esther looked out towards the audience. "Then it's a good thing you won a washer!"

~ ~ ~

Vivian had less than three weeks to prepare for her Jubilee trip to Florida. As odd as it may sound, considering her upbringing, she had never flown in an airplane. In fact, she had never traveled outside of New England.

She had already booked a hectic Tupperware party schedule for the entire month of April but luckily, Babs and Stew were going to take over the dates during her five day absence. There were a million and one things Vivian had to do to prepare for the trip, including buying a few lightweight summer dresses, hats and a set of luggage. And Babs was more than eager to tag along giving Vivian advice and fashion tips. Together, like two teenagers getting ready to go to their first dance, the women bopped in and out of stores up and down Main Street like there wasn't a care in the world.

Meanwhile, a black Mercedes Benz was slowly making its way through the center of town. Driving it was an unusually nervous Irene Lawson. Every time she passed someone walking along the sidewalk she slowed her car down to scan them carefully. Ignoring other drivers honking at her, she came to an abrupt stop to avoid running a red light.

"Where the hell is she?"

She rested her elbow on the steering wheel and dropped her chin into her palm, looked to her left and then immediately perked up.

Vivian juggled a large, medium and small carry-on case of matching luggage as she squeezed her way out of Sutherland's Department Store.

Irene illegally pulled a U-turn right there in the intersection while still at the red light. She narrowly missed another car and pulled into Sutherland's parking lot, stopping just short of Vivian.

Frightened she was going to be run over, Vivian dropped the luggage and lunged out of the way as Irene got out of the car. She pretended not to see her daughter and walked right past her to the store's entrance.

Vivian did a double take. "Mother?"

Irene slowly turned around and acted completely surprised. "Vivian? Is that you?"

"What are you doing here?"

Irene looked up at the store's sign. "I'm buying some...Sutherland's."

Vivian awkwardly embraced her as Babs came out of the store loaded down with purchases. She managed to put on her happy face. "Hey Mrs. Lawson, how the heck are you?"

Irene studied her. "Do I know you?"

The happy face instantly disappeared. "Uh...no. No, you don't know me at all." Babs turned to Vivian. "I'll wait in the car. And good luck."

Irene took out a hanky and dabbed her face with it. "Maid 4

said she thought you did a drive-by."

"You make it sound like I'm a hit man."

"You didn't even have the decency to stop and say hello? I've been worried sick, Vivian."

"About what?"

"You! I haven't seen or heard from you since you walked out on me at the Banam Club."

"I've been busy."

"I called numerous times and the phone company said your line was disconnected."

"I lost the house."

Her mother looked at her like she was mad. "What do you mean you lost it? How can someone lose a house? I called Patrick at the precinct and he wouldn't take my call."

"It's Paul and I divorced him." Vivian picked up the large suitcase.

"Hmm, smartest thing you've ever done. Where are you going?"

"I'm flying down to Florida."

"On whose dime?"

"Tupperware's."

Irene had to think for a moment. "You're a Fuller Brush man?"

"No. I sell Tupperware."

"Cosmetics?"

"No," Vivian said with an irritated tone as Irene headed for her car. "It's Tupperware. You're the one who said, 'Plastics, plastics, plastics.'"

"Why would they fly *you* of all people to Florida?" She opened her car door, got back in and slammed it shut.

"Because I'm the top selling regional…"

Irene started the engine cutting Vivian off. "My life is extremely lonely now. Can't you keep in touch with your own mother?"

Vivian was beyond confused. "I'm…sorry. I should have…"

"I'm going to be late."

Vivian pointed to Sutherland's. "What about the department store?"

"Is that what it is? No time for idle chitchat." She leaned her head out of her window allowing Vivian to kiss her cheek, which she did quickly and reluctantly. "A door-to-door salesperson."

"I am not. I host parties."

She shifted the gears. "Thank heaven your father is dead because this would kill him."

Vivian couldn't believe what she had just said.

Irene examined her face. "And that lipstick is all wrong for your skin tone."

She pulled out of the parking lot and sped off as Vivian watched her, completely baffled.

"Mother, you bought it for me."

~ ~ ~

Later that night, Stew was cooking up a storm in Babs' kitchen. He pulled a roast chicken out of the oven and placed it on top of the stove to rest. Then he added butter and cream to a pot of potatoes and started mashing them.

Babs flew down the staircase and noticed the dining room table set for two. "It smells like Thanksgiving."

He looked at the sexy dress she was wearing. "Who is it tonight?"

"You make me sound like a tramp!"

"I could break out into a song about this."

They both laughed as he spooned roasted vegetables onto a platter.

Babs ran to the hall mirror and checked her make-up. "So I met this guy who's divorced, has two grown children and lives in the basement apartment of his mother's house."

"Sounds like a keeper."

Babs stuck her fingers into the mashed potatoes, scooped out a clump and tasted it. "Someday you're going to make someone a great wife."

He slapped her hand. "You just figured that out?"

"How long have you been slaving over this?"

He looked at the clock, took an apple pie out of the oven and placed it on a cooling rack. "Just three and a half hours."

Babs grabbed her coat and handbag. "She's going to love it. Don't wait up for me."

"I never do."

Meanwhile, Vivian was sitting in the upstairs hallway, talking on the phone.

"Darla, this is so exciting. Karen and Paula are interested too, so I can train you all at the same time."

Stew dished the mashed potatoes out into a serving bowl and placed it on the table along with the vegetables and roast chicken. As he was lighting the candles on the table, Vivian hurried down the staircase not even noticing what he was doing.

"Stew, that was another recruit. That's eight this week."

"Great," he said half-heartedly as he saw her open the front closet and take out her coat.

"Sorry I can't stay for dinner. Darla, Karen, Paula and I have decided to start work tonight. Trying to get as much done as possible before I leave for Jubilee. Can I borrow your car?"

Thrown, he hesitated.

"Stew, were you going to use it? I can call one of them and be picked up."

He used all his strength not to show his disappointment. "No. No, I'm not going anywhere." He handed her his keys.

"Thanks a million," she said as she took them from him. "Don't wait up."

She dashed out the door, leaving Stew standing there in a daze.

"I never do."

After a moment, he looked at the table and then blew out the candles.

~ ~ ~

The day of her trip, Babs and Stew drove Vivian down to Boston but it took twice as long as usual because it was raining so hard. They feared she would miss her flight but once they reached Logan International Airport it was a relief to discover that the plane was delayed due to weather.

It was still stormy when Eastern Airlines decided to let the passengers board the plane and prepare for takeoff. Terrified of flying, Babs tried to convince Vivian to wait for better weather but she laughed it off. Vivian had already been through enough hardship in her 25 years that she had developed a rather fatalistic approach to life.

"Babs, if something goes wrong it goes wrong. If I'm going to die, why not let it happen during my first, thrilling flight, through the sky!"

"Honestly Viv, that's just morbid."

"Maybe you should wait," Stew suggested.

"But it would be disappointing not to meet Brownie." Vivian handed her boarding ticket to the airline agent and turned back to them. "You're both being ridiculous. They wouldn't let us fly if it wasn't safe."

Babs and Stew gave each other a worried look.

"Wish me luck!" Vivian laughed as she ran out onto the tarmac.

Everyone boarding the four-engine propeller plane was dressed as though it were the opening night of a Broadway show. The stewardesses all looked like high-fashion runway models and the pilot, co-pilot and flight engineer seemed like they were plucked right out of central casting.

Vivian was beyond excited as she sat down in her window seat.

The plane carried 40 passengers and it was packed full. And once they were cleared for takeoff and the pilot started up the engines, Vivian glanced out of her round porthole window and laughed at the sight of Babs genuflecting and Stew praying.

Sitting just in front of the wing, the roar of the propellers was deafening as they taxied down the runway in the light rain. The man sitting next to Vivian broke out into a flop sweat.

"Are you all right, sir?" Vivian asked.

Whether he chose not to hear her or couldn't, he popped a pill into his mouth, closed his eyes and gripped the seat's armrests with white knuckles.

The plane picked up speed and even Vivian was a bit concerned when she felt the nose of the aircraft lift up, sensing they just weren't going fast enough yet to take flight. Within moments they were air born and instantly the plane bounced up and down and side to side due to turbulence.

Luckily, Vivian wasn't prone to motion sickness, but as she looked around at others suffering in the airplane, she quickly discovered what the little white bags were for.

And once they reached an altitude of 22,000 feet, they were suddenly cruising above the bad weather and into pure sunshine at the remarkable speed of 300 mph.

The stewardesses appeared and the flight turned into a glamorous party, high in the sky. Drinks were poured and delicious food was served as they were propelled towards Tampa, Florida.

Out to the world, the man seated next to Vivian slept through the entire trip. But she wasn't going to miss a single detail. She soaked up the trip like thirsty sponge. Vivian had always marveled at the fact that such heavy ships like this could get off the ground and soar through the air but the beauty and awesomeness of looking down upon the earth from so high up was something she could never have imagined. She loved every minute of it.

And although the landing was a bit bumpy and the runway seemed a little too short as the pilot aggressively put on the plane's brakes forcing everyone to lurch forward, it didn't faze Vivian at all. She was now in sunny Florida.

She knew it would be warm and tropical but she was surprised the moment they stepped off of the plane. It wasn't just hot and humid, the light was brighter and the balmy breeze coming off of the gulf water mixed with the scent of citrus in the air was intoxicating.

After she retrieved her luggage she noticed a woman standing near the exit door holding a large sign.

Welcome to Jubilee

Tupperware

Dreams Do Come True

Vivian was escorted to one of several buses that were full of dealers, managers and distributors from all over the country. The Jubilee attendants were welcomed, filled in on everything that was going to happen during the next several days and were taught the Tupperware theme song as they were bussed the hour and a half trip to the headquarters in Kissimmee.

Vivian was lucky and she knew it. Brownie's invitation to the Jubilee was being paid for by Tupperware. Most others had to pay their own way. A secretary had contacted her before she left and informed her that she was would be staying at the Orange Blossom Trail Motel a few miles away from the celebrations. She would be bussed back and forth each day to all the events. The single story non-air-conditioned units built in a half circle embracing a less than enticing swimming pool were nothing fancy or even worth writing home about but Vivian didn't care. This was the first time she had stayed in a motel, out of town, out of state, by herself and she was ecstatic.

At first she thought the Tupperware song was a bit corny and just kind of hummed along but eventually she got caught up in the excitement everyone was feeling and she started singing out louder than anyone else.

Looking out of the bus window as they traveled inland, Vivian was amazed at how flat the terrain was. Any other person coming down from the lushness of New England would have thought Florida looked as bleak and barren as the moon. Up north the blazing yellow forsythia had already reached their peak while the pink blossoms of the dogwood and crabapple trees were just beginning to open up.

But Vivian found Florida to be fascinating and exotic. The landscape was dotted with trees she'd never seen or heard of before like loquats, mangroves and bottlebrush. Mile after mile, they passed by vast farmlands, orchards full of lemons, oranges and grapefruits and sometimes just…nothingness. Then, as if it were a mirage appearing out on the horizon, Vivian could see the gleaming-white colonnaded building of the Tupperware Home Party Headquarters.

She felt her heart skip a beat as the bus pulled into the parking lot. There were hundreds of people, about 90 percent of them women, making their way down a long pathway bordered by treasure chests, each with a pole extending from it and waving colorful flags depicting names of each of the United States. On either side of the walk were beautiful lakes, which had fountains in the middle of them, spewing giant sprays of water.

At the end of the pathway was the main pavilion, which housed the Pacific Hall, the Midwest and the Gulf rooms. As Vivian, and all the other Tupperware devotees entered the pavilion, their immediate reaction was one of relief. It was air-conditioned. Outside it was 98 degrees with full humidity.

And the first thing she saw inside was the impressive 42 foot long mural titled the *Evolution of Dishes*. Drawn in a contemporary style it depicted the history of dishes, starting with prehistoric times and ended in the present, with Tupperware. And set up farther down the hall was a huge corkboard with a sign above it that simply read:

•*"*•.,,♥,,.•*"*•*WISH LIST*•*"*•.,,♥,,.•*"*•

Like many others, Vivian stood there for a moment trying to figure out what it was for when out of nowhere appeared a beautiful woman, dressed as the Wish Fairy. She wore a ballerina's costume and tutu, her head was adorned with a tiara and she carried with her a magic wand the size of which would have made Glinda the Good Witch green with envy.

As she pointed to a table that had small slips of paper, pencils and thumbtacks, she waved her wand and said to all, "Attach your wish to the official wish list. Make sure you attach your wish."

Everyone, including Vivian, wrote down their wishes and stuck them up onto the corkboard. From there, the Jubilee attendees picked up their nametags and then were escorted to the enormous Pacific Hall.

Vivian entered and found a seat as the master of ceremonies on stage was doing a sort of warm-up act. He was clowning around, telling jokes and the spirit and energy in the room was infectious. When everyone was seated, several women came on stage, stood behind him and suddenly the back curtain opened revealing a full symphony orchestra playing the intro to the Tupperware theme song.

The MC spread his arms as if embracing the audience and encouraged them to join him.

"Come on, everyone, stand up!" he shouted.

Vivian and everyone else in the hall stood up.

"The ladies behind me are going to show you some choreography. When we say head, we all touch our heads, when we say heart, we touch our hearts, when we say toes, we touch our toes…maybe!" The crowd laughed. "And when we say all over me, we jump as high as we can. Ready?" He asked again, louder, stirring up their enthusiasm. "I asked, is everybody ready?"

They all shouted back, "Yes!"

Along with the orchestra they sang out as loud as they could.

"I've got that Tupper feeling up in my head, deep in my heart, down in my toes. I've got that Tupper feeling all over me, all over me to stay!"

Immediately, they broke into another round of the song and cheered even louder at the end. The MC applauded with them as the women on stage exited and he motioned everyone to sit down.

"Thank you and welcome to Jubilee." The audience cheered. "I know you've all been waiting for this moment so let's bring her out now...the woman who encourages and inspires us to be the best we can be...here she is, Brownie Wise!"

The crowd jumped to its feet again, cheering, as she came out on stage. The brown eyed and perfectly coiffed, pewter haired Brownie was decked out in a pink cotton pleated tiered dress cinched at the waist showing off her lean figure. With it she wore her signature pearl necklace and matching pearl earrings.

Vivian was mesmerized. So was the crowd. And it took them quite a while to calm down and sit back into their seats.

Brownie graciously bowed to the auditorium and walked up to the microphone.

"Welcome everyone. As you know, our Jubilees are designed to reward you, our best selling, hard working, loyal dealers, managers and distributors."

The audience applauded.

"Along with games and prizes we also have the Tupperware business class where we teach effective ways of selling product and recruiting people, followed by graduation. And don't forget that over the next few days, the Wish Fairy will be granting wishes."

The crowd reacted again.

"Welcome to the Tupperware Jubilee, where everything begins with a wish." She gestured as she walked off stage and into the audience. "Follow me!"

Like the pied piper, Brownie lead the entire group outside of the pavilion and out onto the south lawn where a huge area of land was sectioned off with fencing. The earth looked as if it had been tilled and hundreds of shovels spaced equally apart were sticking out of the ground. Everyone gathered around as Brownie now spoke through a megaphone.

"This is the Forest Of Spades. Sometimes it takes hard work and a little sweat to see your dreams come true. When I say go, all of you run to a shovel, start digging and see what you can unearth. One, two, three, go!"

A bullhorn blared and under the blazing sun everyone scrambled for a shovel and started digging.

The first woman to find something screamed when she uncovered a small box. The lucky lady opened it up and found a diamond ring inside. Another unearthed a larger box, tore it open and yelled, "Hooray!" when she discovered a toaster.

Farther back, the crowd went crazy when a woman found a mink stole.

With an assistant shading her with an umbrella, Brownie walked around the Forest Of Spades, encouraging them with words of praise as she came upon Vivian.

Determined to find her treasure, Vivian dug like mad, but unfortunately, the area that she was digging in was bit swampier than others causing it to sink farther down. Eventually she hit something hard. Covered in mud, she pulled out a large box and opened it up as Brownie and others watched on.

Vivian stood there confounded as she looked at an odd looking pot. "What is it?" she asked the woman digging next to her.

The crowd laughed as the girl said, "It's a double-boiler."

Vivian looked at again as if it was the most precious thing in the world. "Just what I wanted," she said, absolutely sincerely. "A double-boiler!"

She turned to the girl again and whispered, "What's a double-boiler?"

Brownie leaned in to her assistant and asked, "Who is that girl?"

The assistant got close enough to look at her nametag. "Vivian Lawson."

Brownie smiled as scores of people continued to dig through the mud.

~ ~ ~

The Jubilee was a constant buzz. During the day there were seminars, classes and demonstrations. At night there were dinners where everyone dressed up followed by concerts, entertainment and gift giveaways. Each night, as the bus returned Vivian back to her room at the Orange Blossom Trail Motel, she was so exhausted that not even the helicopter-sized mosquitoes zooming around all night long could waken her from her deep and restful sleep.

On the second day, Vivian and hundreds of others, sat at classroom style desks concentrating hard on the tests they were taking. A bell went off and everyone passed their papers forward.

And that night during a candlelit graduation ceremony with organ music playing in the background, Tupperware attendees were handed out their diplomas.

The classes were helpful and informative but the graduation had a much deeper impact on many of the students. For some, this would be the first graduation they had ever experienced in their lives. But as each person went up on stage to receive their diploma, Vivian became more and more worried that maybe she hadn't passed the courses. Now, the last person left, she looked nervously amongst the crowd wondering how she would handle the embarrassment.

Brownie paused before she spoke. "And last but not least, our valedictorian, Vivian Lawson."

Vivian was so surprised, she struggled to make it up the steps to the stage.

Brownie embraced her and whispered into her ear. "I'd like to speak with you privately."

Confused, Vivian moved a step back as Brownie handed her the diploma. "Yes, your Highness...I mean, yes, Ma'am."

She laughed. "Call me Brownie."

~ ~ ~

The next day, Brownie walked arm-in-arm with Vivian through the gardens on her 20-acre estate located about 15 minutes south east of the headquarters.

"It's all so beautiful," Vivian said as they parted huge palm leaves and walked out onto a lush, bright green grassy lawn that stretched towards East Lake Toho.

"I'm lucky to have 1,900 feet of frontage property," Brownie said. "Not to mention three horses, two dogs and a wonderful prankster of a teenage son." She gestured out into the water. "And my very own Isla Milagra."

Vivian squinted to see what she was pointing at. "Who is Elsa Millagraw?"

Brownie laughed. "Isla Milagra. It's my island. Translation means – Miracle Island. It's pretty wild right now and over-grown. No one lives on it and it's covered with Carolina willows, bald cypress and oaks dripping with Spanish moss but I'm going to tame it and turn it into a sanctuary for all of you. A place to contemplate, give thanks and make more wishes."

"Isla Milagra," Vivian softly repeated. "I love it."

"And welcome to Water's Edge."

Again, Vivian was at a loss. "You mean we're at the edge of the water?"

She laughed. "No, I mean my home." Brownie gestured down the shore and there stood a Spanish style mansion with a red tiled roof. "Rumor has it that it was originally built for a some 1930s

Hollywood star whose name escapes me, but they never moved in."

They continued to walk arm-in-arm towards the house. "Vivian, you've sold an awful lot of Tupperware in a very short period of time, my dear. Come on in."

The foyer to Water's Edge was magnificent. Decorated with Italian statues and giant ferns, sweeping staircases invited one up to the second floor suites.

"It's magnificent," Vivian whispered.

Of course Vivian was no stranger to living in opulence, however her mother's decorators, whom were the most expensive one could find in New England, designed a house that felt cold, sterile and museum-like. There were rooms in her house she was not allowed to enter, rooms she had never seen in her life. But to Vivian, Water's Edge felt like a home, one full of life and begging for entertaining. She sensed that Brownie had handpicked each treasured item herself because she loved and wanted to be surrounded by them.

They walked into the massive living room that was tastefully decorated in floral prints, imported rugs from all over the world and on the walls hung original and eclectic modern art. Much of the furniture was handmade of bamboo or wicker and shipped up from Key West.

Brownie walked Vivian over to a pair of French doors and dramatically opened them up revealing a large swimming pool.

"It's inside your house?" Vivian exclaimed.

"Isn't glorious? It's filled by a spring and then runs back out into Lake Toho. Refreshing but mighty cold."

They passed by a grand piano and into the dining room that had a table 15 feet long and then on into Brownie's state of the art, ultra modern kitchen. The cabinets were all made of capitol steel in a cheery peach color and the floor was covered with blue linoleum.

The first thing Vivian noticed was an appliance built into one of the counters.

"Is this?"

Brownie smiled. "An automatic dishwasher."

Vivian caressed it. "I've never touched one before." Then she noticed the cooking range. "Electric, too?"

Brownie nodded as Vivian fantasized never having to deal with another gas stove for the rest of her life.

"Come with me," Brownie said as she headed back towards the staircases.

On the second floor, they passed by Brownie's home office that had an executive style desk paired with a giant peacock fan chair and then they reached her bedroom. Vivian hesitated as Brownie entered the pink room fit for a princess. She turned back, waving to her to follow, as she opened a set of mirrored doors.

"This is *my* sanctuary," Brownie giggled as she invited Vivian into her dressing room.

Larger than most people's bedrooms, there were racks upon racks of dresses, blouses, skirts, suits, slacks and coats all organized according to color and season. There were two separate walls of built-in shelves for hats, handbags and shoes.

Brownie continued as Vivian followed her, awestruck. "Few people have been in here."

"I'm honored," Vivian whispered.

Brownie walked her down to the far end of the dressing room. To the left was an ornate vanity with a large beveled mirror. To the right was a floor to ceiling mirror mounted to the wall and seated in front of it was a professional stylist's make-up chair.

Brownie turned and looked at Vivian. "You've had some hard times."

"Yes, but Tupperware has changed my life."

"Vivian, let's change it just a little more." She sat her down in the chair. "You and I have a lot in common. Before my dreams came true I was a struggling single mother with an eighth grade education." She spun the chair so Vivian could see herself in the mirror. "You could go far in this company. But you must remember that when representing Tupperware, you are first and foremost a lady." She ran her fingers through her un-styled hair. "You're a pretty girl. We just need to bump things up a notch."

A hairstylist, make-up artist and wardrobe assistant all seemed to magically appear as if from out of thin air.

Brownie looked at Vivian through the mirror. "I think you should go blonde."

Vivian looked at her doubtfully. "With my brown eyes?"

"And we need to find the right make-up for your complexion."

The professionals descended upon Vivian before she even had a chance to object.

~ ~ ~

After washing, coloring and cutting Vivian's hair they carefully wrapped it up into large rollers. While her hair was drying, they spun her around so she couldn't watch and they did a complete overhaul of her make-up routine.

When finished, they brushed out her hair, turned her back around and she honestly didn't recognize herself. Instantly tears started to flow.

"No. Stop it!" Brownie laughed. "Your make-up will run and your eyes will get red and scrappy!"

Vivian leaned forward, looking at herself in the mirror. "Can that be me?"

"It is you my dear."

"My hair looks a little bit like Grace Kelly's."

"Very much like Grace Kelly's! You look stylish and pulled together. Beautiful but accessible and relatable."

"You think?"

"I know."

Vivian studied herself in the mirror. "I…I…I look pretty."

Brownie helped her out of the chair as the stylists left her dressing room. "When a Tupperware lady goes out she wears a pretty dress. The one you have on is OK, but you must shine. Let's get you out of this and try some of my things on."

As Vivian unzipped her dress and stepped out of it Brownie immediately was drawn to her waist.

"What is this?" She reached out to touch the bizarre looking scar that encircled her torso.

Vivian recoiled. "Oh, please don't."

"Does it hurt?"

She laughed sarcastically. "Not physically."

"What happened?"

Vivian hesitated and then decided to share with Brownie the incident with the Wedgewood. She related the story in such an unemotional, disconnected way that it moved Brownie immensely. She sensed Vivian was trying her hardest to deal with it, in the only way she knew how. And that was by not dealing with it at all.

Vivian stared at it through the reflection in the mirror, fearfully. After all these years it still appeared red and raw as if it had happened a week ago. "I never touch it except to quickly brush over it as I am bathing." Feeling safe yet vulnerable in Brownie's presence, her eyes suddenly misted up. "I...I hate it."

"Vivian, we all have scars, inside and out. I think it's important that you embrace the burn. If you can't learn to love it, at least respect it. Be proud of it. It's your badge of courage. It is there as a reminder to you, that at a very young age, you suffered a horrific accident but you survived. You were given a second chance."

She smiled as Brownie embraced her in a very motherly fashion.

"Vivian, it's important to share with the world both your inner and outer beauty. You are your own treasure chest, don't hide away your precious jewels." Brownie took Vivian's hand and walked her over to the endless number of dresses hanging on racks. "Now let's find you some pretty things."

Luckily, both women were a size 6/8 and as if she had won a shopping spree on a game show, Brownie loaded Vivian down with dresses, gowns, coats, hats, shoes, bags, anything Brownie could get her hands on. With the help of the stylist team, Vivian ran behind an antique Italian dressing screen while Brownie flicked on a switch. From hidden speakers mounted in the walls, Frank Sinatra could be heard singing *Three Coins In The Fountain* as Brownie sat down in the stylist's chair and watched Vivian model each outfit.

With her hair swept up in a French twist, Vivian first emerged wearing an exquisite mauve silk strapless Jean Louis gown with a matching velvet bolero jacket and opera length gloves.

Brownie's hands flew to her mouth as she jumped to her feet she was so taken by her beauty. "Brava!"

Vivian twirled around once, laughed, curtsied and flew back behind the dressing screen.

Next, she came out in a single-breasted gray Chanel suit with two stand pockets and an inverted box pleat at the center front of the skirt. It was paired with a cream satin blouse that had a large bowtie. And to complete the ensemble, she wore black suede pumps and toted a matching handbag. She looked like a million dollars. Vivian walked up and down the dressing room as Brownie spun her around, nodding approvingly.

"Chic! Impressive!"

Vivian dashed behind the screen for her next change.

With her hair simply brushed back, Vivian came out in a stunning creation inspired by a dress worn by Grace Kelly in *Rear Window* and designed by Edith Head. It had a fitted black bodice with a deep V cut down to the bust in the front, and in the rear, to the small of her back. With an off the shoulder neckline and cap sleeves, its full skirt was hemmed at mid-calf. With it she wore a white chiffon shoulder stole and black high-heeled shoes with asymmetric straps. She stood before Brownie holding a narrow black patent leather belt.

She paused a moment and then slipped the belt around her waist and fastened it tightly. Vivian took a deep breath and smiled at Brownie as she got up and hugged her.

"Good for you, Vivian. And by the way, you look like a princess."

Vivian ran behind the screen for one more change. Finally she emerged with her hair curled tighter, similar to Brownie's and wore a simple but elegant silk dress with a geometric pattern in blue and white. The close fitted top had a square collar and capped sleeves while the skirt was full and flared. On her feet she wore matching blue pumps and around her neck, a short strand of pearls.

Brownie stepped back admiring her. Side by side, they glanced at each other in the mirror and smiled.

"Now let me think," Brownie teased, "where have I seen this look before?"

They both doubled over in laugher.

The icing on the cake was that Brownie let Vivian keep everything she tried on.

~ ~ ~

That night Brownie paced the stage of the Pacific Hall in a tight waisted floral chiffon dress. She had praised and congratulated the attendees for all the hard work they had accomplished. And with the help of the Wish Fairy, she had also handed out an assortment of gifts, which included a complete living room set, a bedroom suite, a one-week Paris vacation, and an entire wardrobe for a family with 12 children.

"As we close this year's Jubilee we must reflect. It is a time for gratification and it is a time for Thanksgiving. We would not be human if we were not gratified at the success we have had. We would not be very worthwhile human beings if we were not thankful for it. Thankful not for luck, in which I have very little confidence, but thankful for the strength which has been given to our hand and the ingenuity that has been given to our minds and the willingness with which our spirits have been enriched." The audience applauded. "We have only one more wish to grant, one more magical selection. Everyone, close your eyes and concentrate on realizing your deepest desire."

The auditorium became silent as all visualized what they needed most in their lives. A soft buzzing sound came over the PA system indicating that the Wish Fairy was in the hall. She tiptoed on point down the center aisle wearing her tutu and waving her magic wand and stopped a row past Vivian's and lifted her wand. She took a step back and gently touched Vivian's shoulder. She opened her eyes and screamed as the crowd went wild.

Dressed in the last outfit she had modeled for Brownie, she ran down the aisle to the stage and almost tripped running up the side stairs. Brownie beamed as she handed Vivian the piece of paper she had tacked up onto the corkboard the first day of Jubilee.

"Vivian, please read to everyone what your wish was."

She was so excited her hands trembled, making it hard for her to read her own writing.

"My husband left me, I lost my house and I have no automobile. I'm fine on my own, a home I'll buy someday but I really could use a car to get to my Tupperware parties."

The audience was silent.

"Let Vivian's wish be granted."

Brownie gestured to the curtains behind her as Vivian turned around. The red velvet drapes opened and there, slowly spinning on a platform, was a car.

"Vivian, it's a brand new, two-tone pink and white Chevrolet convertible. It's motoramic!"

Vivian's knees buckled and Brownie had to catch her from falling. Vivian whispered to her. "A 1955?"

Brownie smiled, shaking her head. "56. With a V8 engine."

"The only V8 I've ever had was in a drink!"

Brownie embraced her again and walked back to the microphone as Vivian touched the beautiful car. "And if Vivian accepts this offer, we would like her to star in our next Tupperware television commercial!"

The audience went crazy as Vivian managed to walk over to Brownie. She looked at her in disbelief. "Me?"

Brownie nodded. "And your answer is?"

She looked out to the auditorium as the crowd roared and then back to Brownie.

"Yes! Yes! Of course, yes!"

NINE

A STAR IS BORN

Vivian was back in Abbot only a few days before Tupperware had her on a train zooming down to New York to shoot the commercial. She was allowed to bring a travel companion and of course Babs nominated herself. Meanwhile, Stew, with help from the women Vivian had recruited as dealers, took care of the parties she had already pre-booked.

Neither of them had ever been to Manhattan and Babs was determined to make the most of the trip. As the train pulled into Grand Central Station she jumped to her feet.

"An all expense paid vacation to New York City," she squealed as she started pulling down her suitcases from the overhead rack. "Who would have thunk?"

"This is not a vacation," Vivian corrected her as she carried her sensibly sized suitcase in one hand and make-up case and handbag in the other. "You're my chaperone. This is a business trip." Vivian made a frightened face. "And I have to make a television commercial."

The doors to the train opened and Vivian gracefully stepped

out onto the platform as Babs was lost behind. Caught in a stream of travelers eager to disembark, she tried to drag out not one, but two large overstuffed suitcases, two smaller cases, a make-up case, a handbag and a hatbox, as hurried male commuters pushed and prodded their way past her.

"What happened to chivalry?" Babs shouted, as she was the last to exit the train car.

She caught up to Vivian just as she was about to enter the Grand Concourse. They thought Boston's South Station was impressive but this was simply jaw-droppingly magnificent. The expansive structure was 125 feet high, 275 feet long and 120 feet wide. The elaborately decorated astronomical ceiling was painted in gold leaf on cerulean blue oil and the celestial stars were illuminated with light bulbs.

Gold chandeliers hung from the ceilings adding another flare of opulence but it was the giant sunbeams streaming in through the 60-foot high arched windows at either end of the terminal that truly made it feel like a religious experience.

Vivian and Babs spun around drinking in the experience without speaking a word. Suddenly, a stampede of people who had discovered that their departing train had switched tracks, nearly trampled them down running to their newly announced gate. Once the coast was clear, Vivian and Babs took a deep breath and headed towards the west side exit.

Vivian took out a piece of paper from her handbag. "It says here that the hotel is only 17 blocks and one avenue away. Do you want to save some money and walk it?"

"Their money?" Babs gave her a ludicrous stare and pointed to her luggage.

"Taxi!" Vivian hollered as they exited Grand Central Station.

~ ~ ~

Tupperware spared no expenses and put Vivian up in a deluxe

room at the Plaza Hotel. As they made their way through the lobby Vivian glanced all about, as if she were searching for someone.

"Do you think she's here, right now, in this lobby?" Vivian asked, all excited.

"Who?"

"Eloise!"

"From the children's book?"

"Actually, I mean Kay Thompson who wrote it. They say she lives here and that Eloise is really fashioned after her goddaughter, Liza Minnelli."

"Stew would faint right now. I don't know what we should do first. Peek into the Oak Room or have some tea in the Palm Court or look! Celeste Holm is performing in the Persian Room tonight. Should we book a table?"

"Babs, how about we check-in first?"

The luxurious suite was on the eighteenth floor and faced north over Central Park South. Inspired by the Louis XV style of French décor, the spacious room had two beds plus a sitting area. Refined elegance is how Vivian's brochure described the room and the rose marble and gold-fixtured bathroom was fit for a queen. In fact, many a queen had stayed there.

The moment the girls had tipped the white-gloved bellboy, the phone rang. Brownie's secretary in Florida was making sure everything was to Vivian's liking and then broke the news to her that the schedule they had sent, describing when and where she had to be, had changed. A lot. In fact, she no longer had that first afternoon to explore the town. The forecast called for rain the next few days and they had to do an exterior location shot. Vivian was going to be picked up shortly and driven out of town, into the suburbs, while it was still sunny out.

Babs threw herself upon her bed like a petulant child. "I didn't come all the way to New York City to go to Jersey!"

"Then stay here," Vivian said as she grabbed her make-up case and ran into the bathroom. "You don't have to go."

Babs sat up. "Really?"

Vivian stuck her head out. "Really." She disappeared and then reappeared just as quickly. "But promise me you'll be careful. Don't get yourself into any trouble."

"What is that supposed to mean?"

In no time, the front desk called up and said a car had arrived for Vivian and she flew around the hotel room gathering what she thought she might need. Meanwhile, considering how early they had to get up to catch the morning train, Babs decided to take a quick catnap before heading out.

"There are a million and one things we have to do, Viv, so when will you be back?"

"Unfortunately I don't know," she said as she grabbed her coat. "Go out. Have fun. But don't do anything I wouldn't do."

"Well then, I might as well just stay here in the room all day!"

"Very funny. Wish me luck," Vivian said as she headed out the door.

"You don't need it. Break-a-neck!"

She stuck her head back in. "I think that's break-a-leg."

"I'm sure you'll break something."

"Gee thanks!"

~ ~ ~

A limousine drove Vivian and a production assistant, a young man who looked liked he could still be in high school, out to Short Hills, New Jersey. They crossed over to the West Side Highway, drove all the way down till they hit the Holland Tunnel and then crossed the Hudson River to Jersey City. Just past noon, the highways were clear and they made it to the house they were shooting at in just about 45 minutes.

During the drive Vivian was told that she would only have to speak several lines on camera. They would shoot the outside scene and all the interior ones that day and into the night. And then the next day, she would record a voice-over for the entire commercial in a New York City studio.

"What a relief," Vivian confessed to the assistant. "Acting and walking and talking all at the same time. I feared it would be like rubbing my head and patting my stomach."

"You'll do just fine, Evelyn."

"Vivian," she corrected him, looking a bit worried.

Short Hills was beautiful. In fact, the lush and hilly landscape reminded Vivian very much of Abbot. The house chosen was a split-level and there were a dozen or so actresses already on set as well as all of the production team, the director and two representatives from Tupperware, waiting for Vivian. If she hadn't been so rushed and thrown into the organized chaos, she surely would have choked and possibly let her nerves get the better of her. Knowing that the entire success of the commercial was sitting heavily on her shoulders was already daunting, but the way it panned out, she hadn't the luxury or the time to worry. She just had to do it.

Before she could say hello to anyone, she was whirled into hair, make-up and wardrobe as the director went over the first shot of the day.

Back at the hotel, Babs took a quick shower after her snooze, put on a pair of beige Capri pants, matched it with a black cashmere sweater and sensible flats and she was out the door.

Upon exiting the hotel's main entrance she was facing Grand Army Plaza. Directly in front of her was the opulent Pulitzer Fountain, which had a bronze statue on top and water bubbling down it like champagne flowing over tiers of a wedding cake.

To the left and north, across 59th Street, she could see the glimmering gilt statue of General Sherman being guided by an angel. And surrounding both monuments were beds of thousands of white tulips, all in full bloom.

Suddenly, Babs heard the clip-clop sound of hooves as a horse and carriage emerged from Central Park. She was tempted to jump in and take a ride but decided she wanted to wait and share the experience with Vivian. But beyond the carriage was a vendor's cart with a giant colored umbrella, which reminded her that she hadn't eaten a thing all day. She carefully ran across the street dodging cars, buses and bustling people and saw that he had giant soft pretzels, hot dogs and sodas for sale.

She bought a dog, smeared mustard across it and just a few yards away, walked into Central Park through the southeast entrance. Below street level and surrounded by trees, the pond, full of ducks and geese, was a welcome relief to the hustle and bustle of the city. She sat down on a park bench and looked back over her shoulder and saw the Plaza peeking its head out from above the trees. "How perfect is this?" she whispered to herself.

As she chowed down her hot dog she made mental notes of everything she wanted to see. *Must go downtown to Greenwich Village.*

Babs had recently read a pictorial article in *Coronet Magazine* titled, *Judy Holiday Tells Her Story Of Greenwich Village* and it enthralled her. Judy talked about Washington Square Park, the Theatre de Lys with its experimental plays, the art galleries and of course, the bohemian nightclubs and coffeehouses.

Oh, and we have to see the Statue Of Liberty, the Empire State Building. Suddenly she paused and said out loud, "Damn this dog is good." She got up and walked back towards the vendor as she finished her last bite. *Maybe we'll have time to take a sightseeing boat ride around Manhattan and sit in the audience of a live television show over at Rockefeller Center or hop over to Radio City Music Hall and see the Rockettes and take in a movie!*

She reached the vendor's cart and very demurely asked for another hot dog. "They're so yummy," she exclaimed.

The man looked at her blankly. "Really?" He looked down into the tank of murky water the franks were drowning in.

"Really. I think I'll have catsup on this one, please. Oh, and isn't Tiffany's nearby?"

"Two blocks south on Fifth," he said as he fished another dog out.

"Thank you ever so much."

He handed it to her, she gave him the money and Babs was off for the day.

Just like he said, she walked two blocks south on Fifth Avenue and across the street there was the store she had always heard about. But right next to her on the west side of the street was Bergdorf Goodman's. She had to make a decision. Tiffany's or Bergdorf's? It was Tiffany's first, then Bergdorf's and then the rest of Manhattan. She waited for the light to change as she enjoyed her second hot dog and then made her way kitty-corner across the intersection to the famous store.

"This was too good," Babs said as she wiped her mouth with her napkin and gazed at the window display full of priceless jewels. *Hmmm, would a third dog be too much?*

~ ~ ~

Close to 9:00 P.M. that night, Vivian dragged her exhausted body into the hotel room. With the lights out and the shades drawn, she assumed Babs was out on the town. She flicked on the switch and then heard a painful moan from one of the beds.

"Babs?" Vivian whispered.

With her entire body enshrouded with bed covers, she managed to eek out, "Awwwhhh."

Vivian rushed to her side. "What's wrong? Are you hurt?" She pulled back the blanket and sheets revealing a very sick Babs.

She looked up at Vivian and covered her mouth as she shot out of bed and into the bathroom. Vivian stood at the doorway and watched as she threw up in the commode.

"You're sick?"

Babs nodded.

"What happened? Did you over do it today?"

Babs splashed water on her face and then glanced in the mirror. "Ugh. I didn't do *anything* today. Except…"

"Except what?"

"Three vendor hot dogs, a glance at Tiffany's and food poisoning."

"Aww geez."

Looking like she was about to expire, she barely made it back to her bed. "The house doctor came up."

"And?"

"He's really cute. And single too!"

"You don't stop, even on your deathbed."

"He said just to give it time and drink plenty of fluids."

"You poor kid."

"But you have to go out and paint the town."

Vivian finally took off her coat. "I'm too tired and I have to be in the recording studio by 8:30 A.M. Do you mind if I just order room service and watch some television?"

Babs covered her head with the blanket. "Whatever."

Vivian picked up the hotel menu. "Do you want something to eat?"

"Noooo!"

~ ~ ~

Even though she had only had a little fruit for lunch, Vivian was so exhausted, she had no appetite. Brownie had called to check-in and told her that the advertising agency and the director were thrilled with her work on the shoot. And then she asked if Vivian was eating enough. So she forced herself to order some soup and a Caesar salad with grilled salmon.

In no time, room service was knocking at her door. They rolled in an elegant silver cart draped with linens and set up dinner for her in the sitting area of the suite near the television. She tipped the waiter and asked Babs if she wanted some of the food.

A muffled "Ugh!" emanated from the body buried in the bed.

It was about 9:20 P.M. when Vivian turned on the television set and changed the channel to CBS to watch the *I Love Lucy* show. She sat down and started nibbling at her food but unfortunately, the episode airing was titled, *Lucy Does A TV Commercial.* On the show, Lucy had just started her rehearsal for the live performance for the Vitameatavegamin tonic containing 23 percent alcohol and it was clear, things weren't going to go as planned. As Lucy finished one rehearsal and then started the next, she clearly became more intoxicated and even more side-splittingly funny.

This was the last thing Vivian needed to watch the night before doing her voiceovers for the Tupperware commercial but it was so darn comical she couldn't stop watching. "At least I'm not doing it live and in front of an audience," she whispered to herself.

~ ~ ~

Shortly after dinner, Vivian managed to brush her teeth before passing out into her bed. She was so tired she never heard the multitude of times that Babs had to get up and rush to the bathroom during the night. In fact, not until the concierge's desk rang the phone with a 6:30 A.M. wake-up call the next morning, did Vivian stir from her sleep.

The entire day that Vivian was voicing over the commercial, Babs continued to suffer, venturing out of bed only to run to the bathroom.

Around 7:00 P.M. Vivian opened the hotel door and found Babs watching television wrapped up in her blanket.

"How are you feeling?"

"I'm alive."

"If it's any consolation, it poured all day." Vivian looked at her watch. "We only have this night left. Can you risk going out?"

"No. But I will."

"Brownie made a reservation for us at the 21 Club just in case."
Babs dragged her body into the bathroom. "Let me take a shower."

~ ~ ~

The rain had stopped. It was such a gorgeous spring night when Vivian and Babs stepped out of the Plaza that they decided to walk to the restaurant instead of having the doorman hail a cab for them.

Arm-in-arm, they strolled down Fifth Avenue, window shopping and people watching till they reached 52nd Street and made a right. Halfway down the block was the four-story 21 Club and its famous line-up of 33 painted lawn jockey statues standing guard on the second floor balcony.

Vivian and Babs had reservations in the famous Bar Room whose walls and ceiling were adorned with toys and sports paraphernalia donated by famous patrons. When they walked in, all eyes turned to them as diners quickly started whispering to one another. It may have been because Vivian was wearing a gorgeous rose-colored dress with matching peplum jacket designed by Lilli Ann. It clung to her narrow waist and then flared out dramatically at her hips. Or maybe it was because Babs squeezed into Brownie's Chanel suit and accessorized with an oversized pair of dark sunglasses, which she never took off.

As soon as they sat down, a bottle of Veuve Clicquot champagne was brought to their table with a note from Brownie and the Tupperware Company, thanking Vivian for all her hard work.

When the waiter came to take their order, the only thing Babs asked for was a bowl of consume and a side of cigarettes.

Vivian looked at her. "Talk about a liquid dinner."

"Hey, I'm thirsty. I've been driving a porcelain bus all day." Babs pointed to the plate of food in front of Vivian. "Besides, you're eating for both of us."

"I'm actually starving." Vivian had ordered the filet mignon and Lyonnaise potatoes and managed to scoff down every bit of it.

"So, dahling," Babs said in her best Tallulah Bankhead voice, "how was your day?"

"I'm not certain. I couldn't get a read on the director. I had to do so many takes today to get it right."

"Brownie implied they all liked it."

"We'll see."

Babs looked around the room. "Hey, look at all the attention we're getting. Isn't this grand? They all think we're somebody."

"Yeah, but who?"

They both giggled as they toasted with another glass of champagne.

After dinner the girls hopped into a cab and headed down to the Empire State building and zoomed up to the 102nd floor observatory where for dessert they feasted on a 365-degree view of the New York City skyline.

"It's simply breathtaking, isn't it?" Vivian whispered.

"Yes, he is," Babs said out of the corner of her mouth as she drooled looking at the gorgeous man standing next to them.

"I'm going to have to put a muzzle on you."

"Ruff! Ruff!" Babs barked.

~ ~ ~

During the next two months Vivian kept up a hectic schedule of throwing parties and training new dealers. The commercial was finally going to premiere during an episode of *Make Room For Daddy*. The top public relations executives, including Brownie, were so pleased with the end result and Vivian's performance that they launched her into a huge print campaign for the company. Jockeying her back and forth between Abbot and New York and occasionally off to the burbs for a location shoot, Vivian was already appearing in newspapers, magazines and roadside signs as *the* Tupperware lady.

The night of the commercial's airing, Gloria and Debbie came over to Babs' house to share in the excitement. *Make Room For Daddy* was almost three-quarters of the way through and Vivian, who was sitting next to Stew on the sofa, had to remind herself to breathe, she was so terrified. The sound was off on the television set as everyone waited anxiously.

"Vivian," Debbie exclaimed, "did you see the billboard out on Route 1?"

Gloria stretched her arms out wide. "You're bigger than life!"

"It makes me look fat, doesn't it?" Vivian asked.

Stew looked at her like she was crazy. "Hardly!"

Babs hollered from the kitchen. "Is it coming on soon?"

"It has to be," Debbie said looking at her watch. "The show's almost over."

Vivian started fanning herself. "Is it hot in here? I'm so nervous."

Stew awkwardly put his arm around Vivian and hugged her. "You know, Viv," he struggled with his words, "I really miss... you...when you go off to do the promo stuff and..."

Vivian skirted the awkward moment and looked at everyone in the room. "I miss all of you too."

Babs came running in with a bowl full of popcorn and sat down next to Vivian.

Gloria pointed to the television. "This must be it!"

Stew jumped to his feet and turned up the volume.

As the sitcom faded to black they heard a full orchestra begin to play and then Vivian appeared on screen. The girls in Babs' living room squealed as they saw her wearing a simple but stunning Jonathan Logan cobalt blue shirtdress cinched at the waist. She had on a short strand of pearls and white kid gloves as she took a stack of Tupperware bowls out of the backseat of her car.

She paused and smiled at the camera, so natural-like. "Hi there. My name is Vivian Lawson and I'm a Tupperware lady."

Everyone screamed again as Stew flung his hands. "Shush!"

The camera followed Vivian up the walkway to the front door of the house in Short Hills.

"This is my friend Pat's house and things are popping inside. Why don't you come in and join the party?" Vivian motioned us to follow her.

They cut to Pat's living room where 15 women, some seated, some standing and others looking at a display of Tupperware products on a table were all chatting with each other and smiling.

Vivian joined the group of women admiring the Tupperware as she voiced over the commercial.

"The girls love getting together to meet old friends and make some new ones."

The commercial cut to Vivian standing before all of them while holding up a Tupperware bowl in one hand and the lid in the other.

"Then I give a demonstration."

She gracefully put the lid onto the bowl.

"Watch me show them how to use the patented Tupperware seal. See, you put the lid on tight then press down the center and lift the seal a bit on one side."

Vivian did so and they heard a whoosh sound.

"Hear that? That's Tupperware's airtight promise to lock in flavor and lock out air."

They cut to Pat's kitchen where Vivian pointed to a bowl of lettuce. She picked up a leaf and snapped it in half.

"So salads keep their crunch."

She jiggled a bowl.

"And gelatin keeps its jiggle."

She picked up a pitcher full of water.

"Since Tupperware can't spill or leak…"

Vivian turned the pitcher upside down.

"You can store it any which way in your freezer or refrigera-tor."

They showed Vivian slipping a bowl sideways into a stocked freezer full of Tupperware.

The next scene, Vivian walked into Pat's living room and spoke directly to the camera.

"Plan to attend or host a Tupperware party soon."

She held up a copy of the Yellow Pages and pointed to a Tupperware ad.

"Just look us up, under plastics."

With all of the female extras smiling behind her, Vivian held up a small wrapped present next to her face.

"And don't forget, every hostess receives a valuable gift from," and she paused for a brief second, "Tupperware."

All of the women converged around Vivian as they chattered away, admiring the Tupperware. The music swelled to a finish and the commercial faded to black.

Everyone in Babs' living room cheered.

"Does my voice really sound like that?" Vivian asked.

They all laughed and congratulated her as the phone rang. Vivian jumped to her feet. "I'll get it."

"I bet it's Hollywood calling!" Babs exclaimed as Vivian went into the kitchen.

She turned back and looked at her. "Oh, stop it."

"Hello?" she said as she picked up the extension.

Vivian turned away from the group as she heard the person's voice on the other end, just as the doorbell rang.

Babs ran to the door, opened it and standing there was a burly United Parcels Service man.

"Delivery for a Miss Vivian Lawson."

"Vivian, Santa's here," Babs shouted as Stew, Debbie and Gloria dashed outside to see what it was.

Babs held back, catching a glimpse of Vivian's face. She looked so pale, she wondered if she were speaking to a ghost.

"How did you know I was here?" Vivian asked in a serious tone. She saw Babs watching her and waved her to go outside.

Babs joined the others as the UPS man unloaded a large box onto a hand truck.

"What is it?" she asked.

"Just a brand new color TV," Gloria said, nonchalantly.

They all laughed as Babs opened the garage door. In there was a boxed refrigerator, a washing machine and dryer and a large record player and radio console squeezed in beside Vivian's Chevrolet convertible.

Babs gestured to the far corner. "Maybe you can stuff it in there next to the rest of the loot."

Vivian slowly came out of the house and made her way over to Babs' side.

"Viv, who was that?"

She had trouble even saying his name. "Paul. He congratulated me on the commercial and..."

"And what?"

"He wants to see me."

"Well, you're not going to."

"No," Vivian said, unconvincingly.

"Vivian!"

"Of course not."

The deliveryman grabbed his clipboard with the paperwork. "I just need the lady's Jane Hancock."

Stew gestured to Vivian. "She's the one right over..."

He cut him off. "I know which one is Miss Lawson."

He handed her the clipboard and as she signed it he pulled out another piece of paper. "Miss Lawson," he asked sounding like a shy kid about to ask for his first kiss, "any chance you could sign this too?" Vivian looked puzzled. "If my wife found out I met you and I didn't get your autograph I'd be sleeping on the couch for the next year."

Everyone laughed as Vivian took the paper and pen. "Of course, what's her name?"

"Carolyn."

This was Vivian's first time ever doing this so she had to really think about what to write. "Dear Carolyn, Wishes do come true! All the best, Vivian Lawson."

She handed it back to him and he hopped back into his truck.

"Thanks a million!" he hollered as he drove off.

Vivian waved. "No, thank you!"

Debbie grabbed Vivian by the shoulders. "You're famous now!"

Gloria pointed to all the boxes and the car in the garage. "With *everything* you could ever wish for."

Vivian laughed. "Everything except a house to put it in."

TEN

LONELY HOUSE

Vivian's schedule became even more exciting but hectic in the weeks that followed. The Tupperware commercial was such a huge success that the corporation signed her to a three-year contract. Of course Brownie would continue to be the corporate face of the plastics company but Vivian would be the media spokeswoman. Receiving a salary of $30,000 per year, Vivian would also take home any monies made from creative bookings. Her commercial was airing nationally all the time and bringing in huge residuals. She was also paid extra for the print modeling and radio advertisements she did for the company.

Plus, she didn't quit her day job. She had created a small army of Tupperware dealers who were working beneath her. Stew was actually running this end of the company, virtually single handedly. The occasional parties Vivian did find time to host were so popular that she had to move them to auditoriums to handle the crowds of people who not only wanted to buy the Tupperware and share in the fun but also meet Vivian in person.

When many looked at the timeline of events, they flippantly

said her success happened overnight. But overnight? Hardly. Vivian had been paying her dues since she was born. It's just that when the returns started coming in, they came in faster than anyone could have imagined. Vivian herself was the first to admit that none of this was or could have been planned or thought out. It was fate and a lot of hard work.

Getting up the nerve to stand in front of groups of strangers and figure out how to motivate them to buy product took brains, guts and determination. And from being invited to Jubilee to Brownie taking her under her wing and offering her the commercial to it being a tremendous success, Vivian had experienced synchronicity in its truest form.

Up until now it could still take an actor in Hollywood years to develop notoriety and a fan base. But with the advent of television the entire process was sped up. With over 10 million homes watching TV in 1955, a person could become a star overnight. And that's exactly what happened to Vivian. She was now a household name and rolling in cash.

This meteoric rise would have been difficult to handle even for someone who already was a celebrity, someone used to the limelight and being paid handsomely for it. But for Vivian, this was obviously virgin territory hence there were bound to be some challenges for her along the way.

~ ~ ~

Babs watched Stew as he put his clothes into the bedroom dresser with a long face.

"Well, at least you're getting your room back, Stew."

"She's taking me over to see the house in a bit." He stopped what he was doing and turned to her. "Aw Babs, I gotta pull out the stops and impress her somehow so I was thinking..." he went to his closet, "I really need to dress sharp." He pulled out a very nice blue shirt. "Like this?"

He put it up to his chest. Babs stood back and looked at the shirt and then grabbed it from him and threw it onto the bed.

"Peacocking."

She went to his closet and rifled through his clothes.

"Pardon me?"

"You have to start peacocking and master the art of dressing for attention. Like a peacock strutting his feathers. It reeks of arrogance and all us girls flip over it." She examined the last shirt hanging in his closet. "No, there's nothing in here." She spun around and looked at him. "I have an idea. My closet!"

Stew watched her as she dashed out of the bedroom. "This doesn't feel so good."

~ ~ ~

On July 18, 1955 Disneyland opened to the public and one of the most adored and iconic Disney characters ever created, Cinderella, was prominently featured at the theme park. Five years earlier, the film was released and the beloved song, *A Dream Is A Wish Your Heart Makes*, was destined to remain a favorite for generations to come. What had happened to Vivian's life was not unlike Cinderella's, but along with her theme song, there should be a cautionary warning: be careful of what you wish for.

On this same glorious July afternoon in Abbot, Vivian turned left off of River Road and onto Clark in her pink Chevrolet with the top down. Stew was sitting in the passenger's seat wearing one of Babs' outrageously loud Hawaiian print shirts and a powder blue Sherlock Holmes hat that was just a bit too small for his head.

His hand flew up to the hat as the wind blew it to the back of his head. "Oops, almost lost it!"

Vivian looked at it. *Pity.*

She stepped on the gas as the incline of the hill increased and Stew gripped the armrest, feeling his body being pressed back into the seat.

"I think you might be going beyond the speed limit, Viv."

"Can't wait for you to see it," she hollered as they zoomed past the mansions.

They reached the top of the hill, Vivian slowed down to make a left onto Osgood and then pulled over to the side of the road.

Stew looked at her wondering what she was doing. "Is the car OK?"

She smiled at him and then gestured to across the street.

He looked. "Yes. The Shepherd house."

"And what do you see in the front lawn?"

"A sign that says…" he squinted, "sold."

Vivian grinned from ear to ear.

He put two and two together. "You? You bought the Shepherd house?"

She nodded proudly.

"But I didn't even know it was for sale."

"It wasn't. I made them an offer they couldn't refuse." She opened the car door and got out.

"But Viv, it's so large."

"I've always been madly in love with it."

Together they crossed the road.

"Can you really afford something like this?"

"I just signed on for three more commercials."

The two of them stood up against the waist high ancient stone wall surrounding the 1716 colonial house.

"Don't you think you'll be lonely in that rambling thing all by yourself?"

"Never!" She opened the white picket gate. "I love it. I love it. I love it! I can't believe it's mine. And I did it all on my own."

Stew watched her with a worried look as she twirled around on the front lawn like a child ecstatic at the news of getting her first puppy.

~ ~ ~

Anyone looking closely at the Shepherd house could recognize that it had great potential, potential for being a money pit. And Vivian wasn't blind to this. She was just in love. And being a true Abbotonian, Vivian was respectful enough not to play with the structural integrity and history of her new home.

She had the 25 double hung, 12 over 12 paned windows painstakingly stripped of peeling antiquated paint, repaired and freshly recoated for a crisp, clean look and preservation of the wood. Most of the panes had been replaced over the centuries but some of the original wavy glass was still intact.

The massive central chimney that provided the house with its five fireplaces was repointed. The 50 black shutters were literally falling apart and the next strong wind that came along would certainly blow the rungs away like featherweight matchsticks. Also, the roof on the back end of the house needed to be replaced.

There was a cement in-ground pool that was drained so that minor cracks could be repaired before being repainted and filled with water again but the pool house with an additional two bedrooms and bath was in good enough shape that she didn't need to deal with it at the moment.

But the white clapboards on the exterior of the house were a big issue. Due to long term neglected termite infestation, much of the siding had to be replaced. Simultaneously, the interior wooden structures had to be chemically treated to rid the home of these pesky intruders.

But as expensive, time consuming and threatening as these insects were, nothing was peskier to Vivian than Paul. Since first seeing her on television, he continued to bother her. At first it was a call here and there asking if they could get together. Then the calls became more frequent. He never really said what it was that he wanted to talk about. Instead, he just insisted that he needed to see her in person, in public. The pain he had caused was fresh enough to give her the strength to keep him at bay but occasionally, upon leaving the house, she had the dreaded sense that he may be lurking in the bushes about to jump out at her.

Vivian welcomed her numerous business trips out of town, which gave her a break from his annoyance and reduced her chances of possibly running into him in town. It was also a relief from the tremendous amount of dust and chaos associated with the restoration.

As she continued to bop back and forth to New York doing more photo shoots, magazine interviews and her next commercial, she was also buying up furniture to fill this enormous house. Like Brownie, she wanted to surround herself with beautiful things and create a home that begged for entertaining.

The one room that she did choose to completely gut and bring up to date was the kitchen. Its most recent makeover was about 20 years earlier and the day the workmen tore out the old gas stove Vivian cheered.

The color scheme for the kitchen was pink, crème and black. State of the art stainless steel Highpoint appliances were installed throughout the open concept workspace. On one wall were Vivian's side-by-side refrigerator and freezer with the stylish rounded corners and circular chrome center handles. Upper and lower pink cabinets paired elegantly with the beige and coral speckled Formica countertops and there was a dishwasher installed next to the stainless steel sink.

On the adjoining wall was a floating double oven mounted between two black columns and next to that was an expansive pink floating counter with four electric cook tops. Each one being a separate unit, they actually folded up into the wall when not in use. Matching the cabinets and counter tops, the floor was a speckled tan, crème and pink linoleum. The kitchen was clean, sleek and nothing anyone had ever seen before.

But, although she had restored the house to its original splendor, Vivian was determined not to fill it with stuffy and dated décor. Obviously influenced by her trip to Water's Edge, Vivian took a big risk and decorated her New England colonial mansion in a shocking "Floridian" style.

~ ~ ~

It was on a warm late September day when Vivian threw herself an early housewarming party. The south facing siding had yet to be replaced and the shutters were still in the process of being restored but Vivian wanted to celebrate while the weather was still warm and the pool swimmable.

Out on the back patio, Babs, Debbie, Gloria and Vivian, who was wearing a knock-off of the Marilyn Monroe white halter dress she wore in *The Seven Year Itch*, sat around the poolside table with a slew of magazines scattered all over it.

Babs threw up her arms. "Whom are we waiting on?"

"Hush," Vivian said putting her index finger up to her lips. "I don't want to jinx it."

Stew came out of the house carrying a tray of cocktails. "Another round, ladies?"

Gloria grabbed a glass. "Stew, you're looking more handsome than ever, I must say."

He actually blushed. "Finish that drink and I'll look even better."

They all laughed as Debbie pointed to the pile of magazines. "Viv, your Tupperware ads are in *Better Homes and Gardens, Good Housekeeping, Redbook, Charm, McCall's...*"

Vivian held up the copy she was looking at. "And *Modern Woman.*"

Debbie took a large gulp of her drink. "When do you have time to breathe?"

"I don't," Vivian sighed. "I just did a radio show in New York and have to fly down to Kissimmee for the planting ceremony."

Babs wasn't sure she heard her correctly. "The what?"

Stew pulled up a chair and sat down. "Brownie is doing a festival tree planting marathon at headquarters."

"To symbolize the nurturing of fruitful lives," Vivian said, very dramatically.

Babs held up her glass towards the pool and then to the house and toasted. "Here, here! Your fruit is so ripe it's about to fall off the tree!"

They all cheered as the doorbell rang. Vivian almost knocked the table over as she jumped to her feet.

"Be right back," she said as she ran into the house clutching the copy of *Modern Woman*.

As Vivian crossed through her living room she strategically placed the *Modern Woman* magazine onto the coffee table and quickly paused to check her hair and make-up in the mirror hanging over the fireplace mantle. The doorbell rang again. She rushed to the front foyer, stood next to the Italianate statue and giant potted fern tucked under her spiral staircase and took a deep breath. After a quick look up to the heavens for good luck, she opened the door.

Standing there with her back to Vivian while surveying the front yard with a critical eye was her mother, Irene.

"I was afraid you weren't coming, Mother."

She continued to stand with her back to her daughter. "I wasn't going to. But Maid 4 is whining about chest pains again. I told her she should see a specialist at Mass General but oh no, she insists on seeing her old doctor, and I mean *old*, up here at Bon Secours. So I dropped her off for her check-up and…" Irene finally turned around and saw Vivian for the first time since her makeover. "Oh my! The hair? The make-up? And what in God's name are you wearing? Where is my Vivian?"

She laughed, nervously. "I'm still here."

"You look…" Irene struggled with the word, "good dear. You look…good."

Vivian tentatively gestured for her to enter.

"You bought the Shepherd house?" she asked, incredulously.

Vivian stood a little taller. "Yes I did."

Irene walked into the living room, which was decorated almost identically to Brownie's. Pastel floral prints covered two easy chairs and matching bamboo sofas faced each other in front of the fireplace. And in between them was a giant glass coffee table with a weathered driftwood base. Modern paintings and sketches adorned the walls and the draperies in all the windows matched the print on the furniture. And anchoring the room was a large rattan rug.

It was all very beautiful and obviously expensive but the disconnect between the tropical décor and the colonial house was completely jarring.

Irene entered the room and unconsciously ran her finger along the top of the fireplace mantel and checked it for dust.

She looked at her finger. "Hmmm."

Vivian followed behind her as she walked about the living room. "I've got four bedrooms and two and a half baths, Mother. Oh, and in the kitchen I've installed an automatic dishwasher and out back is a beautiful pool and barbecue pit."

"You give her a dollar and she thinks she's a Rockefeller," Irene mumbled.

"What was that?"

"Everything is picture perfect and in its place. Just like a doll-house."

Vivian wasn't sure if that was a compliment or not. "You like the way I've decorated it?"

"You did it yourself?"

"Yes," she said, proudly. "I call it," she paused and giggled, "early everglades."

Irene looked at it critically and whispered under her breath, "I'd call it early awful."

Vivian reached for the cigarette box sitting on the coffee table and offered her one. "Mother, I'm going to appear in some more commercials for Tupperware."

Irene ignored the cigarettes and headed for the front door. "You're acting now?"

Vivian grabbed the *Modern Woman* magazine. "Ah, I was hoping you saw me on television."

"I may have caught the tail end of one of the advertisements."

Vivian waited for some sort of reaction, approval or disapproval but Irene just opened the front door herself and stepped out.

"My friends," Vivian said, pointing to behind the house, "are all out by the pool sipping cocktails and mingling. I was hoping you'd…"

Irene headed for her car as Vivian followed her.

"I've appeared in several magazines, Mother. Including your favorite, *Modern Woman.*" She held the magazine out to her but Irene declined to take it as she went around to the driver's side and opened the door.

"I stopped reading that silly thing years ago."

Vivian glanced into the car and actually saw a copy of it lying on the passenger's seat.

"Well, I think Daddy would be proud of me."

Irene was unable to hold back her true feelings. "Your father would be disgusted with your ostentatious behavior."

"My what?"

"The man hated the nouveau riche." She got into the car and slammed the door shut.

"But…"

She started the car and stuck her head out the window. "I hope you're saving some of this money. What if Tupperware's just a flash in the pan? Goodbye Vivian. I have shopping to do."

Defeated, Vivian stared at her as she pulled out of the driveway and Gloria and Debbie came out of the house.

"Sorry we have to leave," Gloria said, giving her a hug.

"Thanks for the housewarming gifts."

Debbie embraced her. "Viv, will you be at Monday's regional meeting?"

"Not this month. *Home Companion* is coming over for an interview and photo shoot."

"Hoity-toity!" Gloria laughed as they got into her car.

"Remember us little people!" Debbie hollered as they pulled out of the drive.

Vivian waved to them and entered the house as Babs and Stew walked into the living room.

"I have to get inventory papers," Stew said as he headed to Vivian's den.

Babs walked over to a painting on the wall and squinted at the signature. "Must be expensive cause I can't pronounce the name. Everything here looks pricey."

Vivian lit a cigarette. "It is."

"You've made it baby. The house, the toys, the money."

"And I owe it all to Brownie."

Babs couldn't believe what she just heard. "Don't you think someone else deserves a little credit?"

"Of course, Babs," she said rather arrogantly, "you've been a great help."

"I'm not talking about me although that is true." She gestured to the den. "Stew. None of this would have happened without him." Babs dragged Vivian by her arm into the foyer and brought her voice down low. "And you do realize he's crazy about you?"

Vivian started to laugh. "Stewie?"

He came out of the den with both arms full of folders and seeing neither of them in the living room, he walked towards the front door.

Babs poked her with her finger. "Don't you dare laugh."

Hearing them, he paused behind a life-size statue of some naked Greek God whose name he could never remember.

Babs continued in a hushed whisper. "Stew is a catch."

"I have an image to think of now."

"And Stew would cramp your style?"

"He's been dressing funny and acting weird. I'm sure Brownie would want me to be seen with a man a bit more…sophisticated."

Truly appalled, Babs raised her voice hoping Stew could hear her. "Someone's beginning to believe all her own press hype. And the generous guy that did everything in his power to get you back up on your feet is now socially unacceptable?"

"Keep your voice down. I'm not sure he and I are a perfect fit."

"So now you want perfection?"

"I'm not interested in Stewie because he's…" she struggled to find the right word as he moved closer so he could hear. "He's…"

Babs sank into her left hip and glared at her. "Is the word you're searching for…leftovers?"

Having heard enough, Stew stepped out from behind the statue, rushed by them, managed to open the front door on his third try and made a beeline to his car.

Vivian called out to him. "Stewie!"

Babs took a few steps and then turned back to her. "Be careful of the wheel of fortune, Vivian. It always spins." She looked her up and down and then gestured to the halter dress. "And who said Marilyn Monroe wasn't relevant?"

She walked out the door, slamming it in Vivian's face.

~ ~ ~

Later that night, Vivian stood in one of the spare bedrooms upstairs that she had transformed into a dressing room and walk-in closet. Gowns, suits and outfits were lined up on racks like perfect little soldiers and wafting up from the living room could be heard the hypnotic and tropical song, *Quiet Village.*

She glanced at herself in the mirror and admired the black silk blouse paired with gold floral brocade Capri pants. She slipped on a floor-length matching hostess coat, turned left and then right and smiled approvingly as she walked over to her dressing room table.

Stocked with all the "right" cosmetics, Vivian sat down at the vanity and with the precision of a brain surgeon she carefully applied the make-up exactly as she was taught to. She picked up her half-empty glass of wine, took a large swallow and then exaggerated her black eye liner and added an extra layer of fire engine red lipstick. She grabbed the glass and headed out of the room.

Vivian gracefully descended her spiral staircase just as the exotic song was finishing. She walked through her living room to her Emerson phonograph radio console, flipped the LP and stacked another record on top, to drop after *Jungle River Boat* had finished playing.

She lovingly ran her fingers across the state of the art piece of entertainment furniture and took a survey of her room. She adjusted the drapes hanging in the front windows and made sure they puddled perfectly on the floor, realigned a painting by a millimeter to ensure it was straight and fluffed the pillows on the sofas before heading into the kitchen.

She looked through the window of her electric oven at the Swanson's TV dinner cooking, refilled her glass of wine and perused through the stack of magazines she had been featured in. When the timer went off, she took the dinner out of the oven and transferred the fried chicken, corn, mashed potatoes and brownie to an elegant plate of china. She picked up the plate of food and glass of wine and as she headed to the dining room she paused briefly, looked back at her electric dishwasher and smiled.

Vivian's formal dining room table was set for one. She put down the plate of food and the glass of wine and lit her silver candelabra of five candles. She sat down as *Unchained Melody* dropped onto the turntable and she listened to it, not touching a morsel of her food. When the song finished, she continued to sit there as the needle scratched against the LP. Her superficial enjoyment of her evening and belongings was beginning to fade.

She picked up the plate, carried it back into the kitchen and scraped the food into the trash. Vivian refilled her glass with wine and walked back into the living room. Bored to tears and feeling more lonely than ever, she shut off the record player and turned out all the lights out except for one on an end table next to the sofa.

She set her glass of wine down, curled up on the sofa, looked at her copy of Herman Wouk's *Marjorie Morningstar* and unenthusiastically picked it up. She opened the book to where she had left off but slowly her gaze drifted off across the room, focusing on nothing.

Sometime later, all the lights were out in the house. Moonlight shone in from the French doors going out to the patio and all that could be seen was Vivian's silhouette as she continued to sit in the same position on the sofa. She brought a cigarette up to her lips, inhaled and the red tip glowed in the darkness.

ELEVEN

YOU MADE ME LOVE YOU

A month had passed and although Stew continued to run the operations of Vivian's Tupperware division in Abbot, he had managed, with the help of assistants, not to see or speak with her during that entire period of time. It tore him apart inside but he sensed, with Babs' strong encouragement, that it was the best thing to do.

Vivian was OK while working, which was most of the time but late at night when she was home alone or in a hotel room, she ached for Babs' company as well as Stew's. During those moments of reflection, Vivian couldn't really understand what went wrong. She had a job and a purpose, she had the money, the house, the clothes and everything else but she had also lost the two real and only friends she had.

Vivian had just arrived home from a whirlwind trip to New York City, which included doing a live Tupperware commercial on *The Perry Como Show*. At this point, she was pretty self-confident. Memorization of lines she didn't find too difficult but hitting marks and knowing exactly when the camera was on and which one to look into and remembering not to talk too quickly and to bring her voice down into her lower register, was all a bit unnerving. For Vivian, doing the show was definitely filled with an air of excitement laced with terror. What if she goofed? What if she blanked? What if a fly flew into her mouth?

She was a bit shaky when they first went on the air, with her upper lip quivering a bit. And she stumbled over a line halfway through but Mr. Como was delighted to meet her and the advertising hot shots for Tupperware, present on the set, were very pleased with her performance.

Back in Abbot on a Saturday afternoon and not knowing what to do with herself, Vivian got into her car and headed into town. As she turned onto Clark Road and passed the other mansions, it dawned on her that she had forgotten to decorate her front door with an autumnal wreath. With that realization, she had something to do.

She coasted down the hill and with no train approaching, she plopped across the tracks and over the wrought iron bridge across the Drake River. Taking a left onto Mill Road she zoomed up the steep incline effortlessly with the help of her V8 engine in the Chevrolet and the late October sun gleamed off of South Church as she coasted into the center of town.

She casually looked up at the Abbot Movie House as she passed by.

THE SEVEN YEAR ITCH
starring **MARILYN MONROE** and **TOM EWELL**

Coming Up Next

SUMMERTIME
starring **KATHERINE HEPBURN** and **ROSSANO BRAZZI**

Once on Main Street she searched for a parking place but none were available around the Town Florist shop. She took a left onto Chester, passed the Colonial Candlepin Bowling Alley whose lot was full and then pulled in next door to Demoulas grocery store.

While walking past the bowling alley on her way back to Main Street, she noticed that Babs' car was parked out front. She paused and then walked up to the front windows, peered in and saw her bowling with Stew. Sensing she was the last person in the world they'd want to have interrupt their game, she chose to walk on to the Town Florist.

Inside, Babs was about to take her next turn as Stew sat at the scoring table. She grabbed one of the grapefruit size bowling balls and casually positioned herself for the throw. She looked around to see if any men were watching as she haphazardly tossed the ball down the lane and then posed in several different alluring positions. She walked back towards Stew when they all heard a loud crack as her ball hit the candlepins. Stew dropped his head onto the table. She got a strike.

Babs turned around and looked at it, totally surprised. "Wow! Another one! Stew, it's not my fault. I wasn't even paying attention."

"That's what makes it even worse," he moaned. He dragged himself away from the table dreading his next turn.

He picked up a ball and then from the foul line he walked back three large steps. He turned around and faced the pins, blew on his ball for good luck and rubbed it with the sleeve of his shirt. Stew said a quick prayer, stuck his butt way out as he bent his knees and focused his eyes on the middle pin. He took one, two, three steps with the ball swinging back and released it with all his might. Two feet down the lane it skidded into the gutter, again. Totally flustered, he turned around and saw Babs flirting with the guy in the next lane.

Stew sat down, ripped off his bowling shoes and slipped on his loafers.

"What did you get?" Babs asked, picking up the pencil.

"If you had been watching you'd realize. Zero, zilch, nada!"

He grabbed his coat and headed out the door with his hands flailing.

"Hey!"

Outside, he impatiently leaned against Babs' car waiting for her to come out.

"Stew," she shouted, as she walked over to him.

"Babs, what did I do wrong?"

"Maybe you'd do better with big balls?"

He gave her a look. "No! I mean with Vivian."

She got into the driver's seat as he went around to the passenger's.

"It's not you."

Thoroughly frustrated, he slumped into the car as she started it up. "I'm so pathetic. I like her more now than ever. I worry if she's OK. I wonder what she's thinking about. I watch the clock counting the minutes till I can see her again. She rejects me and I still want her." He rubbed his temples as she backed out of the bowling lane's parking lot and took a right on Chester. "I don't feel so well. Maybe I'm sick."

"*You're Just In Love.*"

Without missing a beat he said, "Ethel Merman in *Call Me Madam.* Babs what should I do?"

She turned right again onto Main Street. "Obviously my advice isn't helping."

"You know what? I'm just going to tell her exactly how I feel."

Babs smiled at him as Vivian saw their car approaching her as she walked along the sidewalk. Afraid of them stopping and tearing into her again, she held her giant wreath of colored oak leaves, jack-o-lanterns and twigs of bittersweet up in front of her face.

~ ~ ~

As soon as he got home, Stew pulled out of Babs' driveway in his car, drove down River Road, took a left onto Clark and hit the gas pedal with a huge smile on his face. He knew this was the right thing to do.

He sped up the hill talking out loud to himself. "Viv, I have to tell you…" He shook his head. "Vivian, I think you know… ugh…"

He leaned forward trying to help his car get up the hill faster and then conscientiously glanced at his speedometer and slowed down a bit. "Viv, ever since we were kids…"

As he struggled to figure out what to say, he reached the top of Clark Road. At the intersection he paused, looked to his left and could see Vivian placing the festive wreath over the large brass knocker on the front door.

Self-confident and ready, he put on his left blinker, looked both ways and just as he was about to pull out onto Osgood, an aqua and white two-tone Ford Fairlane cut him off. Stew couldn't believe his bad luck and timing as he watched Paul speed into Vivian's driveway, screeching his tires. Stew made the turn and pulled up along the shoulder of the road just out of their sight.

Vivian spun around when she heard the rubber tires squeal and her body stiffened up when she realized it was Paul. He got out of his car wearing his police uniform and swaggered up to Vivian's front door. Stew was too far away to hear what they were saying but felt he was ready to save her if need be.

Vivian stood on the top step with her arms folded as they engaged in conversation. She then gestured for him to come inside. Paul shook his head no and appeared to be pleading about something. Vivian shook her head and opened her front door. He cautiously moved closer to Vivian and then slipped into the house quickly. She followed him in and shut the door.

Stew was stunned. He sat in his car for a few moments trying to figure out what had just transpired. The only conclusion he could come up with was that Vivian wanted him back. He shifted the car into forward, carelessly made a u-turn, after making sure no cars were in sight, and zoomed off hitting his fist on the steering wheel.

Inside Vivian's house, Paul stood tentatively in her front foyer. Astounded, he looked first at the nude statue and then up the spiral staircase.

"Wow," he said. "This is all yours?"

She stood in the living room staring at him. "No, I'm just a squatter."

"Vivian, we could have talked about this outside."

"I don't want to give nosey gossipmongers in this town any more ammunition. They're doing just fine on their own."

"Well, I don't want you throwing anything at me that could kill."

"Don't give me any ideas." She picked up a glass candlestick from the fireplace mantel as he cowered, covering his face with his forearm. "Paul, what do you want?"

"I just want to talk to you sensibly, calmly."

"About what? You got your goddamn divorce."

"I just...I just want to have dinner with you."

There was something in the tone of his voice, something that shifted in his body language and for a brief moment she saw the old Paul. The Paul she fell in love with, the kind and sweet version. Her hand still gripping the candlestick, she slowly lowered it to her side.

Paul continued. "I've been thinking about you a lot, lately."

Thoughts and emotions started to swirl through her mind. *He's come back on his knees? This is unreal. I hated what he did to me but...do I still hate him? I'm successful now but what's the point if I have no one to share it with?*

"Vivian, I want..."

Intuitively, the fist with the candlestick rose up again and Paul stepped back fearing she would throw it.

"Dinner! Please, let's do dinner. Tonight. DeQuatro's." He

reached for the front door and opened it. "Please Vivian." He stepped through the doorway. "Meet me there tonight. 8:00 P.M. You...won't regret it." He gave her a half-smile and then left, shutting the door behind him.

Vivian stood there dumbfounded.

~ ~ ~

Stew was so angry he couldn't see straight. Instead going back to Babs' he just kept driving. He was so out of it that he was shocked when he saw the pink neon lights blinking ahead.

Danny's
Polynesian Restaurant
and
Tiki Lounge

That meant he had been driving south on Route 1 for at least 30 minutes without even knowing it. Stew swerved into their lot, parked the car and jumped out. He ran into Danny's and headed straight for the lounge.

With the walls covered in grass mats, giant imitation Polynesian carved totems supporting a thatched ceiling and red leather banquettes embracing the room, this establishment was a tropical classic. People came from all over the North Shore to savor the flaming pu pu platters and took their chances with the Molten Mona. Riskily named after Danny's mother-in-law and served in a ceramic mug in the shape of a bare-chested hula dancer, the libation included a lethal mix of light rum, dark rum, sloe gin, peppermint schnapps, coconut crème, pineapple juice and ginger ale. And the bonus was, anyone consuming more than five Molten Monas was offered a free taxi ride home.

But the main draw at this tiki lounge was the entertainment. In the center of the room was a raised circular platform covered with a thatched roof where an extraordinarily talented jazz quartet of Chinese musicians played their hearts out. It consisted of a sax, trumpet, bass violin and Danny leading them on the piano.

It was 4:15 P.M., happy hour had just started and there was a scattering of people seated throughout the room. The quartet was just finishing up a rendition of *Mister Sandman* as Stew paid the bartender for his Molten Mona and sat down at a table in front of Danny. Unlike most people, Stew drowned his sorrows in alcohol *and* show tunes.

"Mister Stew," Danny said, leaning down to him. "You not look so good."

"Ah, I don't feel so good either."

"You need a dose of medicine?"

"Not sure if it would help."

Danny leaned into his microphone and addressed the patrons. "Mister Stew, everybody, you want to hear him sing?"

They all applauded as he pushed the giant umbrella, orange and pineapple slices to the side of his cocktail and took a big gulp of Mona. Stew reluctantly got to his feet, stepped up onto the platform with the musicians and whispered to Danny what he wanted to sing. He turned out to the audience as he adjusted the microphone and sang a very peppy rendition of *After You've Gone*.

"After you've gone and left me cryin', after you've gone there's no denyin', you'll feel blue, you'll feel sad, you'll miss the bestest pal you ever had."

The band shifted from a staccato beat to a slow and lazy one. He plucked the microphone from the stand, stepped down off of the platform and walked from table to table.

"They'll come a time, now don't forget it, they'll come a time when you'll regret it. Oh baby, think what you're doing..."

Stew turned back to the band and brought his arm down fast and they picked up the tempo again as he stepped back up onto the platform for the big finish.

"I'm gonna haunt you so, I'm gonna taunt you so, it's gonna drive me to ruins. After you've gone, after you gone away."

He was actually really good and the audience loved him.

Danny spoke up over the applause. "One more, will do one more?"

"Yes," they all pleaded.

Stew looked out to the people. "We all loved Judy in *A Star Is Born?*"

The audience clapped.

"Hey, if Frank Sinatra can sing this, so can I." Stew took a large slurp of his naked hula girl and then leaned against the piano. He looked out into the lounge as the trumpet started to wail. The quartet picked up on the sultry beat and Stew sang, *The Gal That Got Away.*

He did a fantastic if not melodramatic rendition using staging and hand gestures that he could remember from the movie. And when he was done, the crowd wanted more but this was too much for him. Stew thanked the musicians, walked over to the bar heartbroken and sucked up the last of his girly drink. He signaled the bartender and asked if he could use the house phone and dialed a number.

Danny looked over at him, shook his head and whispered to the other musicians. "Mister Stew is hurting bad."

Stew cleared his throat. "Ah…hello Gloria? Would you happen to be free for dinner tonight?"

~ ~ ~

That Saturday night DeQuatro's was booked solid. Even the bar was stuffed with people smoking and drinking cocktails, patiently waiting for tables. The room echoed with conversation and laughter. Everyone seemed to be having a great time. Everyone except for one man seated in the middle of the dining room.

Paul signaled the waiter for another scotch on the rocks as every head in the joint turned to Vivian as she made her way back to his table from the ladies room. With her hair up in a French twist and wearing black high heels, she looked stunning in a beige knit wool dress cinched at the waist with a thick black belt.

Vivian caught the waiter's eye and mimed writing, indicating she wanted the check.

Paul unsteadily got to his feet and tried to pull out her chair for her, but Vivian was quicker and sat herself down.

She lit a cigarette and studied him. Obviously there was an answer he was anxiously waiting for.

After a long pause, Vivian said without any emotion, "No."

"You're not even going to think about it?"

She looked at her wristwatch. "I did. I went to the bathroom for about five minutes." Vivian took a sip of her martini. "Why would I marry you...again?"

"Because I love you and I want you back."

She looked at him with a smirk. "It's all about you, isn't it?"

Paul downed what was left of his drink.

"Are you going to be able to drive?"

He leaned back in his chair and spread his legs. "Maybe you'll have to take me home."

"I don't know where you live."

"Then we'll go back to your place."

Paul was clearly beginning to slur as Vivian took another puff of her cigarette and blew it in his face. "What happened to Eleanor?"

"You tryin' to change the subject?"

"Heard you were engaged."

Paul leaned in and rested his elbows on the table. "Eleanor...called it off." He grabbed Vivian's hand. She instantly retracted but he wouldn't let go. "Your commercials air all the time." He shook is head as he looked at her. "I just can't get over your transformation."

"And have you changed?"

The waiter arrived with Paul's drink and Vivian was able to free her hand. He placed the leather check holder on the table as she looked up at him. "Thank you."

"You're welcome, Miss Lawson."

As the waiter left Paul took a large gulp of his drink. "You're back to Lawson?"

She gave him a sarcastic look.

He stared hard at her. "Damn you look good. Sure you won't marry me?"

"Very sure." She opened the folder and looked at the bill.

"Last warning. Don't force me to do this."

Vivian laughed at him as she opened her purse and took out her wallet. "Do what?"

He paused. "I'm moving away."

"And that's a bad thing? Where to?"

"The city."

She slipped cash into the folder and closed it. Paul never even made an attempt to offer to pay. "And what will you do?"

"I'm never gonna make captain. Wanna open my own private detective agency."

Vivian ground her cigarette out into the ashtray. "Makes sense. You know how a cheating man thinks."

He paused and then leaned in closer to her. "So, I want half."

"Half of what?"

"Half of what you got."

"I beg your pardon?"

"I wasted the best years of my life with you." Vivian started to get up out of her chair but he grabbed her forearm and wrestled her back into her seat. "You don't want to make a scene, do you?"

"Why in God's name do you think I'd ever give you a single penny of my hard earned money?"

"Because if you don't, a certain Brownie Wise is going to find out that the fresh face of Tupperware isn't so innocent after all."

"What are you talking about?"

Paul slipped his hand inside of his suit jacket. Vivian drew back not knowing what he was doing. He took out an envelope and threw it on the table.

She looked at it hesitantly.

"Go ahead. Take a good look."

Vivian pulled out several photographs and her face instantly registered shock. She hovered over them trying to make sure other diners couldn't see them. "You bastard."

One striking photo was Vivian dolled up like Betty Page, posing in black stockings, garter belt and panties. She was topless but covering her breasts with her hands. The second picture was of her squatting in an old-fashioned washtub wearing just a bra and panties. Her head was thrown back and she's pouring water all over herself with a watering can. In the third, she's wearing a Frederick's of Hollywood lace bra but for a bottom, she's just wearing Paul's holster with her hand on his gun.

Vivian stared at him. "I should have shot you then."

He sneered at her and took the photos back. "I could ask for everything. Just give me half."

She grabbed them out of his hand.

"Vivian, I'll just have more printed up."

She leaned into him. "You forced me to do those photos," she said in a vicious whisper.

"Then you're a damn good actress cause you looked like you were having a great time to me."

"Are you getting pleasure out of this?"

"You give me what I am due and the deal is settled."

"All I ever did was love you and take care of you and dream of having children with you."

He downed his scotch leering at her.

"If only you had asked, I would have told you."

"Told me what?"

"I never wanted children."

"But…"

"I had a vasectomy before we got married."

Aghast, Vivian stood up and threw the rest of her martini into his face. She grabbed her purse and the pictures as his hands went up to his stinging eyes.

At that very moment, Stew and Gloria were just entering the vestibule of the restaurant.

"I wasn't sure if you'd be free on such short notice," Stew said as he helped her with her coat.

"Lord knows my dance card is open," Gloria laughed.

Everyone in the restaurant was watching Vivian cross the restaurant, including the waiter, who had her coat waiting for her. As she slipped him a bill, Stew was just entering the main dining room followed by Gloria.

"Oops," he said as he spun around quickly ushering Gloria back into the vestibule. "It's packed and I forgot to make a reservation."

"We could have a drink at the bar?"

Stew pushed her outside. "I'm allergic to smoke."

They exited DeQuatro's and Stew pulled her down the street. "Gloria, how about I cook. Did you know I'm a gourmet chef?"

"No!"

Vivian came out of the restaurant and headed in the same direction as Gloria and Stew, still not having seen them, as Paul stumbled out after her.

"You can't run, Vivian. You can't hide!"

Vivian turned back to him. "You are so sick!"

Hearing this, Stew stopped and turned back.

"I'm gonna show those lewd pictures to Brownie!" he shouted.

She screamed back. "Fine! Show them to the whole world. I don't care. And take half of what I've got. Hell, take all of it. Just get out of my life!"

Vivian started to walk away as Paul lurched forward and grabbed her coat sleeve spinning her around. She tried to pull herself free as Stew ran towards them. Paul lost his grip and reached for Vivian's coat again but Stew pushed him back.

"Leave her alone!"

Paul stumbled. "Well, if it ain't Mister Goody Two-Shoes. Aw, sorry. Mister Goody One-Shoe."

He reached out for Vivian but Stew put his arm around her to protect her.

"Don't touch her, Paul."

Stew pulled Vivian in the direction of Gloria.

"Or what?" Paul screamed. "You'll shoot your other foot?"

Stew kept walking away from him with Vivian. "Attack me all you want but stop bullying Vivian."

"Stew," Vivian pleaded, "don't get in the middle of this."

Paul caught up to Stew and grabbed his shoulder, spinning him back around. He pulled his arm back to punch Stew but being totally drunk, he lost his balance and stepped off of the sidewalk backwards into oncoming traffic.

Vivian screamed as Stew instinctively dashed out into the street, grabbed him and pushed him back to the sidewalk. Paul stumbled a few feet and then fell, hitting his head on the curb and was knocked out cold.

Vivian turned to Stew and saw a car heading straight for him.

"Look out!" Vivian screamed.

Stew turned around just in time as the car literally brushed by him. He stepped back a few steps and collected himself as a crowd gathered around Paul.

Stew went over to Vivian. "You going to be OK?"

"Yes."

Stew paused for a moment to catch his breath and then joined Gloria.

"Someone call an ambulance!" a man shouted as Vivian watched Stew and Gloria walk off together.

~ ~ ~

Vivian stood next to the automatic coffee dispensing machine in Bon Secours commissary with a glazed look on her face. She couldn't believe that in one day she was proposed to by her ex-husband, then blackmailed and now he was in the hospital. The coffee had just finished dripping into her cup as someone walked up from behind.

"Are you through, Miss?"

Vivian snapped out of her daze. "Yes." The voice sounded familiar. She turned around and it was Irene.

"Mother!"

They both spoke at the same time. "What are you doing here?"

Vivian removed her coffee from the machine as Irene slipped a dime in.

"I'm visiting Maid 4." Irene selected her coffee, the paper cup dropped and the questionable brown liquid slowly dribbled down. "She's up in room 305."

"What do you mean?"

She explained to Vivian that the pain Maid 4 had been feeling in her chest a month earlier was actually the warning sign of a heart attack. And while going through a battery of tests at Bon Secours, she actually suffered heart failure.

Irene grabbed her coffee and blew on it. "She tore some sort of valve and considering her age and weight, they say it's a wonder she's still alive. They don't think she'll make it. And her timing couldn't be any worse," Irene added. "This is my busy social season. Benefits, gala openings, luncheons, bridge parties."

"For the whole month she's been in the hospital? It never occurred to you to call me or visit or share what's going on?"

"No. It never did."

Vivian couldn't find the words, her mother flabbergasted her so much. "Mother!"

"Why are you here?"

"My ex husband."

"Paul?"

"No Mother, his name is…" Irene said it right for the first time ever. "Yes, Paul."

"What happened to him?"

"We're waiting to see. The initial diagnosis is blunt trauma to the head."

"Good. He deserves it."

"Mother! We had been out to dinner and he had too much to drink and was almost hit by a car."

"I thought you divorced him."

"I did."

"And now you're socializing with him? You should be careful Vivian. Clearly you're attracted to abusive people."

Vivian looked away. "God knows it's what I'm familiar with."

"What's that supposed to mean?"

Vivian put up a hand as if to say halt. "I don't want to fight. I don't want to argue. This isn't the time. This isn't the place. I'm confused, I'm upset and a little support from my own mother would be a novel and supportive concept."

"Vivian, if you want empathy go cry on the shoulder of one of your Tupperware ladies. Maybe they can take all your little problems and store them away in a plastic airtight tub and your life will be all hunky-dory again." Irene took a sip of the beverage, made a disgusting face and threw it into the trash.

"Mother, that's it! I've had it. I've had it with the putdowns. I've had it with the criticisms. I've had it with the condescending remarks."

"You're too sensitive. Always have been. Even as a child."

"Mother, children are supposed to be sensitive. And you're mean. I know you don't like me. I fear that you hate me. Let's face it, if we weren't mother and daughter, we'd never be friends."

Babs quietly entered the hospital commissary and listened as Vivian continued.

"Maybe you blame me for something? Or maybe you're just jealous?"

"Ha!"

"I don't know. You never tell me anything. But if you cannot give me the respect that I deserve, if you cannot speak to me in a civil fashion, if you cannot say one positive or encouraging thing to me, then don't say anything at all."

For a split second it looked as if Irene were going to strike Vivian. But her daughter held her ground.

"Mother, is that understood?"

Irene looked at her for a moment longer and then turned and walked away. Babs had to jump out of her path as she stormed out.

Babs went over to Vivian and embraced her.

"You OK, Viv?"

"I think so. Thank you so much for coming. The doctor is still with Paul. Do you want to meet me at the nurse's station on the fourth floor? There's something I need to do."

Babs nodded as Vivian walked over to the elevators. She took it up to the third floor and slowly walked towards room 305. The door was ajar and Vivian was just about to enter when a nun walked up to her.

"Visiting hours are over, my dear."

"Oh, but…I just found out she was here and I'm so worried. If you could just let me see her for a moment. I promise I won't stay long."

The nun paused, smiled and then gestured to the room.

Vivian was about to enter and then turned back to her. "What is wrong with her?"

"Coronary thrombosis."

"Is it curable?"

The nun shrugged her shoulders. "She's on anticoagulants. She must continue to rest in bed."

Vivian took a deep breath and walked in slowly. Maid 4 was lying in her hospital bed with her eyes closed. Not sure if she was awake, Vivian quietly sat down on the chair next to her bed and

Maid 4 turned her head towards her.

"Who's there?" she asked. Her brogue was as thick as ever but weaker and raspier.

"It's me."

Maid 4 focused on her face.

"It's Vivian. Vivian Lawson."

"Oh. Oh my dear Lord."

Vivian touched her hand. "Don't get excited."

"Is it really you? You look so different."

"I hope that's a good thing," she smiled.

"Aw, so nice to see someone smiling for a change. How did you know I was here?"

"I ran into my mother. I'm just so furious she didn't tell me what had happened to you. I would have come to visit. What is her problem? Why does she dislike me so?"

"Sit closer to me before the good Lord takes me away."

"Shhh, don't talk like that."

"There's something I need to get off my chest. It's about your mother." She started to cough.

"Please don't stress yourself."

"Vivian, we're Irish. We don't talk about the past."

"Obviously. I know nothing about my mother. Nothing! I don't even know how old she is."

"Well," she laughed, "you never ask a lady that."

"But she's my mother!"

Maid 4 went on to tell Vivian that her mother was born in Ireland in 1890, which would make her 65 years old. She was the youngest of 11 brothers and sisters. Her father had died shortly after her birth leaving her mother and the children penniless.

At eight years of age Irene was shipped to America, by herself, to work at the Glenallen Mill in Winchendon, Massachusetts. That's where Maids 1, 2, 3 and 4 met her. They were all mill girls. For the next eight years Irene was a threader. Working enormous machines, positioned claustrophobically close together and with the deafening sound of the weavers booming all day long, it was more like prison for the children than work. Every dollar Irene made was sent home to her mother and siblings. All she got was room, board and a few scraps of clothing.

In 1906 Irene was contracted out to the newly opened Lawson Woolen Mills in Abbot. And thankfully, the child labor laws were enforced and life was much different for the workers. Upon laying eyes on Irene, even after years of such hardship, William Lawson thought she was the prettiest girl he had ever seen. A year later, at the ages of 17 and 26, Vivian's parents were married.

"Ah, she was a beauty. Still is. Your father offered her a chance at freedom. Not sure if she loved him, but it was a way out. And once married, she called for us maids to work for her. We couldn't believe we would finally be out of the mills."

Vivian did the math and was astonished to realize that her mother was almost 40 when she was born.

She whispered to Maid 4, "I feel so sorry for you."

"Why?"

"First you're forced to work in mills and then my mother buys you out and turns you into her slave."

"Now don't be disrespecting me."

"Oh I didn't mean to offend."

"I am proud of my job and I am, I was, the best at it."

There was a long pause as Maid 4 closed her eyes. Vivian wasn't sure if she was resting or sleeping, if she should stay or go. And then she started to speak again.

"Your mother never forgave her mother. The day she was farmed out to the mills was the last time she ever saw her and her siblings. And it confuses me, why she passed that anger and frustration onto you, Vivian. Your mother did the best she could with what she had to work with. I'm not saying how she handled you was right, but I don't think she knew any better. Maybe in understanding that, the two of you can have a bit of healing between you."

"It may be too late for that."

Maid 4 tried to sit up and Vivian rearranged the pillows behind her.

"Vivian, the important thing is I know you. I know your heart. You'll break the cycle. One day you'll have children of your own and you'll love them fiercely."

"I know that too. Oh thank you..." Suddenly Vivian stopped mid-sentence and looked very distraught.

"What's wrong, child? Did I say too much?"

Vivian's eyes welled up with tears. "No. No I'm glad you're telling me all of this. I'm upset, I'm horrified because..." She broke down crying. "Because I don't know your name."

Exhausted, Maid 4 signaled for her to come close. "My name is Mary. Mary O'Connor."

Consumed with emotion, Vivian pressed her face against hers. "Hello Mary."

Vivian held on for a moment longer and then realized she had fallen asleep. She quietly got up and left her room. She thanked the nun and walked up the flight of stairs to the fourth floor.

Babs was waiting for her at the nurse's station. "A nurse just told me he was conscious."

A doctor came out of Paul's room. "Miss Lawson?"

Vivian stepped forward. "How is he?"

"We're keeping him overnight. Want to monitor the concussion. The dislocated shoulder will heal on its own. You can see him now if you like."

The doctor continued down the hallway as Vivian turned to Babs.

"Please don't leave. I need to talk to you."

"Do you want me to go in with you?"

Vivian shook her head, walked over to his door and hesitated before she entered.

Paul was propped up in bed with his arm in a sling looking like he had been run over by the car that didn't run him over. She stood by his side and there was a moment where they studied each other.

Paul spoke first. "So, he saved my life?"

"Probably."

"I owe the little jerk."

"Big time. And you're not blackmailing me."

"Aw geez, Vivian."

"You can't because I'm sending the pictures to Brownie myself. I'm sure she'll find them quite amusing."

"Nah, don't do that. I won't use them against you."

She looked at him incredulously. "Did the concussion knock some sense into you?"

He tried to laugh but obviously it hurt too much. "I'm still moving away."

Vivian opened up her purse. "I think that's a good idea."

Paul watched as she took out her checkbook and a pen and started to write.

"Vivian, what are you doing?"

"How much do you need?"

"No. You don't have to."

She stopped writing and looked at him. "No, I don't. But I want to make sure that you do leave and hopefully never come back."

"Well then, maybe a little something just to get me on my feet?" he asked, sheepishly.

She shook her head as she finished writing. "You'll never change."

"You wouldn't consider coming along with me, would you?"

Vivian laughed out loud. "Not on your life."

She handed the check to him as someone knocked on the door and opened it slightly. Vivian went over to it.

Out of Paul's view, a woman whispered to Vivian. "Thank you for calling me."

"Who is it?" he asked.

Vivian opened the door wide and Eleanor rushed in and to Paul's side. "Oh baby, I got here as quickly as I could."

Paul looked at Vivian and smiled as she left the room. She walked over to Babs who was shaking her head.

"Did you mastermind that?"

"They deserve each other," Vivian snickered. "And please accept my apologies."

"For what?"

"I just got a bit off center there for a while."

"Hey, I'm off center all the time and I plan on staying there."

Just then a young, tall, dark, and handsome doctor walked by. He winked at Babs. "Thanks again for your number, Babs. Drinks will be a pleasure."

She winked back. "The pleasure's all mine, I'm sure."

They watched him walk away as Babs elbowed Vivian. "I double checked and made sure he was single."

"You never stop," Vivian laughed. "Say, do you know where Stewie is?"

She shook her head. "I do know that he dropped Gloria off at her house because she called to see if he was all right."

"How will I ever tell him exactly how I feel?"

Babs nudged her. "You'll find a way."

Vivian embraced Babs and rushed out the door.

~ ~ ~

Before she left Bon Secours, Vivian called Babs' house to see if Stew was home but there was no answer. So she drove back into Abbot and checked DeQuatro's restaurant thinking maybe he was at the bar but the waitstaff were cleaning up and the sign said they were closed.

She then traveled on down to MacDonald's and pulled into their parking lot but could clearly see that he wasn't in there.

As she headed back home she passed the movie house and noticed that there was a late showing of *The Seven Year Itch* playing. She bought a ticket and as discreetly as possible, walked up and down the aisles of the theater as the light from the film flickered on the faces of a handful of people smoking cigarettes in the audience. Exhausted and unable to find Stew, she sat down to watch the movie.

It was at a point where Tom Ewell was in the middle of a scene with Marilyn Monroe declaring that pretty girls would never like a man who looked like him. He knew they preferred guys with movie star looks, like Gregory Peck. But Marilyn set him straight. She explained that when at a party, instead of being attracted to the smartly dressed guy that thinks he's God's gift to women, she's drawn to the shy and nervous type that may be sitting by himself in the corner. The kind she could sense is gentle and kind and worried. What she found really exciting was knowing that he'd be tender, nice and sweet to her.

Vivian totally agreed with what she had said. Overwhelmed with emotion, she got up and rushed out of the theatre. Back in her car, she wracked her brain trying to think of where Stew might be and then suddenly it dawned on her. She sped down Route 1 till she saw the giant sign with the pink neon lights blinking and turned into Danny's.

Not surprisingly, the tiki lounge was packed full of late night lovers of good jazz. Danny and the boys were just finishing up a set when Vivian entered and saw Stew sitting at the far end of the bar, with his head hung low, sucking on a Molten Mona. Not seeing her, she quickly went over to Danny and whispered something to him. He smiled and nodded and then told the musicians what Vivian was going to sing.

Knowing she didn't have a strong voice or a good ear, Vivian stepped onto the platform, took a deep breath and walked up to the microphone as the men played a few bars of intro. Nervous, she began to sing quietly and tentatively.

"You made me love you, I didn't want to do it, I didn't want to do

it..."

She looked over in Stew's direction. He didn't turn around but his head came up. With a little more strength and confidence, she continued.

"*You made me want you, and all the time you knew it, I guess you always knew it...*"

Knowing it couldn't be true, he turned around to see who was singing.

"*You made me happy, sometimes you made me glad...*"

Stew got up and walked across the room.

"*But there were times dear, you made me feel so bad...*"

She smiled at him as he made his way through the maze of tables towards her.

"*You made me cry cause I didn't want to tell you, I didn't want to tell you...*"

He stood right in front of her as she nodded and really started to belt out the song.

"*I need some love, that's true, yes I do, deed I do, you know I do...*"

He stepped up onto the platform with her.

"*Give me, give me, give me, give me what I cry for, I know you got the kind of kisses that I die for...*"

Without letting her finish, he grabbed her in his arms and kissed her. The band played on and the audience erupted into ecstatic applause as Stew and Vivian continued to kiss.

TWELVE

MILAGRA

Stew wasted no time in proposing to Vivian and, of course, she said yes. She had a simple but elegant, white strapless silk taffeta gown coupled with a lace bolero jacket designed by Priscilla of Boston. And on January 1, 1956, the small wedding party gathered at Brownie's Water's Edge for the nuptials.

She had held true to her promise. Brownie transformed her wild Isla Milagra into a tropical oasis and when everyone was ready, she had a barge take the bride, groom and guests across Lake Toho to the island.

The weather couldn't have been more perfect. A pleasantly warm late afternoon, the wedding was timed with the sunset and upon disembarking the barge, party members passed through a large archway on the dock with a sign above that read:

ISLA MILAGRA

Tiki torches and a trail of pink rose petals led the way past tables covered in white linen and exquisitely set with imported bone china, Waterford crystal glasses and automatic dishwasher safe silverware. And in the center of every table was a tableau of Tupperware interlaced with flowers native to the island: passion-flowers, wisteria and orange blossoms.

Past the tables, the pathways took the guests to rows of gold painted bamboo chairs where they all took their seats and faced a giant arched trellis covered in pink roses overlooking the water. Under the arch stood Vivian in her gown, Stew in his tuxedo and, having recently become an ordained minister, the officiant of the ceremony, Brownie.

Both Stew and Vivian wanted to keep the ritual simple and light. After they recited their vows and exchanged rings Vivian glanced out into the front row of wedding guests. There was Babs, who winked at her, wearing a tiger print caftan with a mod-est neckline that plunged down to her waist. Next to her were Debbie and Gloria giggling and waving. But when Vivian looked at the woman seated next to Gloria, that's when her eyes misted up. Smiling bigger and more proud than anyone else there was Maid 4, Mary O'Connor.

And surprisingly to many, including Vivian, seated next to her was her mother, Irene. Wearing an inappropriate and extremely warm Balenciaga wool suit, Vivian wasn't sure if her mother was smiling or in great pain. Neither of them knew whether or not their relationship could ever be repaired, but at that moment, there was a quiet sense of mutual respect. As embarrassing as it was for Irene to have Vivian chew her out in public at Bon Secours hospital, she admired her spunk. But of course, she never told her so.

Vivian turned back to Stew who was already bawling which made her start to cry and then Brownie finished up with her most important line of all.

"And it is now, with great honor, that I have the privilege of pronouncing the two of you, by law of the great state of Florida, husband and wife."

Everyone cheered.

"Is there anything you can't do?" Vivian asked Brownie.

"Kiss the bride."

They all laughed as Stew and Vivian passionately kissed each other. And at that moment the Wish Fairy appeared and blessed them with her wand. Her troupe of dancers pranced around while in the background, out on the lake, fireworks started to explode.

And if that weren't enough, Brownie had timed it perfectly so that a motorboat sped by pulling the Tupper-ette water skiing team. A total of 11 women wearing wedding gowns and Tupperware canisters on their heads with veils attached, raced by waving to the crowds. And each one had a letter sewn onto the back of her dress spelling out the words:

JUST MARRIED

Vivian embraced Stew and whispered into his ear, "So much for us keeping it simple."

~ ~ ~

Upon returning home from their Hawaiian honeymoon, courtesy of Tupperware, Vivian's first order of business was to get rid of everything Floridian in the Shepherd house. Some of the artwork they kept but everything else was tagged for their garage sale. And what didn't sell they donated to charity. And then, together, Vivian and Stew redecorated their mansion in the manner to which it was suited. And they took their time to find the things that they really liked and meant something to them. Nothing fussy or pretentious, just homey and colonial. Honestly, that's what the two of them felt most comfortable with. But the one thing Vivian did insist stay the way it was after it was remodeled, was her dream kitchen.

Their other joint collaboration arrived a little more than nine months after the wedding on October 15, 1956. The thrilled parents couldn't imagine naming their beautiful 8.5-pound baby girl anything other than Milagra. For, to both of them, she would always be their miracle.

Vivian continued to be the spokeswomen for Tupperware but tried to make sure, in regard to scheduling, that husband and child came first. She also strongly encouraged Stew to ask for his job back on the force.

He was not only reinstated but shortly afterwards, his boss retired and Stew was named Captain of the Abbot Police Department.

Irene kept her townhouse on Beacon Hill and Mary O'Connor continued to live with her but had to be very careful not to overexert herself. In an ironic and appropriate twist of fate, Irene was now taking care of Mary.

Paul married Eleanor and they moved to California. Inspired by Vivian's commercial and print success, he hoped he could cash in on his good looks and make it as an actor out in Hollywood. Vivian had recently received a letter from Eleanor telling her that as they awaited his big break, he was currently pumping gas at a Shell station. Vivian wasn't sure if he'd ever make it in the movies, but she was glad that he was on the opposite side of the country and hoped he stayed there...forever.

And Babs? She did quit her dental receptionist job and became the manager of Vivian's Tupperware team. She was still single and still hunting for a man, but she also proved herself to be one lifesaver of a babysitter.

On one particular evening, just months after Milagra was born, Babs had the baby dressed in a find she had discovered at an estate sale. Originally made for a large doll, Babs had reworked the silk dress, which had a luscious red rose print on it, into a stunning evening gown. With a cowl neck, skinny matching belt and layers of tulle underneath its full circle skirt, it looked like something Audrey Hepburn would have worn in a high fashion shoot.

While playing on the living room rug, Babs stacked a tower of Milagra's favorite building blocks...Tupperware bowls. As soon as they were up, the baby kicked them over.

"Yay! See? Unbreakable!" Babs said as she clapped her hands. "I love Mi-la-gra! Can you say, 'I love you too, Auntie Babs?' Let's go find out what's for dinner."

Milagra giggled hysterically as Babs picked her up.

Stew had just gotten home from the precinct and was wearing his captain's uniform and Vivian, still in full make-up, had rushed in from a photo shoot. The two of them were whipping up dinner together as Babs entered the kitchen with the baby in her arms.

"So Milagra, I met this guy..."

"Babs!" shouted Vivian.

"Sorry. Mmm, doesn't it smell good in here? What's for din din?"

Stew started to plate the food. "Just herbed pork loin with roasted brussel sprouts and orange glazed mango chutney carrots."

"Just?" Babs asked. Milagra giggled as she put her ear to her lips. "What's that? You wonder how your mom and dad found the time to put together such a delicious dinner with their crazy, busy schedules?" Babs turned to them. "Milagra wants to know your secret."

Vivian and Stew looked at each other, shrugged their shoulders and then held up the Tupperware containers.

Together they laughed saying, "It's leftovers!"

ABOUT THE AUTHOR

ARTHUR WOOTEN is the author of the critically acclaimed novels *Dizzy, Birthday Pie, On Picking Fruit* and *Fruit Cocktail.* He's also penned the children's picture book *Wise Bear William: A New Beginning* and the collection of short stories, *Arthur Wooten's Shorts.* A playwright, his works include the award winning *Birthday Pie,* which had its world premiere at the Waterfront Playhouse, Key West, FL. His one act plays, *Lily* and *The Lunch,* have been produced in New York City and most recently Te Anau, New Zealand. For two years he was the humorist for the London based magazine, reFRESH. Arthur grew up in Andover, MA and now resides in New York City.

www.ingramcontent.com/pod-product-compliance
Lightning Source LLC
Chambersburg PA
CBHW020244150626
46552CB00020B/161